the
start
of
someday

JILLIAN LIOTA

Love Is A Verb Books

Book Cover Design and Layout by Blue Moon Creative Studio

Cover Photo by Studio Firma

Editing by C. Marie

ISBN 978-1-952549-09-0 (paperback)
ISBN 978-1-952549-10-6 (eBook)
ISBN 978-1-952549-11-3 (kindle)

for everyone who hopes
to find love during the holidays

chapter one
abby

"I bet you could bounce a quarter off that ass."

A snort from my left has me turning to look at my best friend, and I can't help but grin at the look of complete exasperation on her face.

"What?" I ask, trying to appear as innocent as possible. "It's true. You know it is." Then I return my gaze to the absolutely fantabulous buns that caught my eye in the first place. "I mean…just look at it."

"Thanks, but I'll pass."

Rolling my eyes at Briar's inability to play with me about this, I continue my attempts at persuasion. "Oh, come on. Having your *own* boyfriend doesn't mean you can't objectively objectify someone else. You're dating, not *blind*," I say, nudging her obnoxiously with my elbow.

Briar narrows her eyes and lets out a long sigh, then finally shoots a quick glance in the direction I've been blatantly staring at for the past minute or two.

"I'd give it a solid six out of ten," she finally says.

My eyes widen, and I seriously begin to wonder if we should just end our friendship right now because...*what*?

"What?" I say, and not quietly. "That is just...completely false. His ass is at least a nine, easy."

Briar scrunches her nose and gives her head a little shake. "Mmmmm, those buns aren't for me."

I look back at the man in question, trying to understand how in the hell we can have such differing opinions.

This guy is built like a linebacker. Tall and muscular and broad in a way that says he can pick a girl up and toss her over his shoulder. I've always wondered what something like that would be like, and I bite my lip, enjoying the way he shifts to dig his wallet out of his back pocket.

"You could not be more wrong," is all I say, finally refocusing all my attention on her. "But I can manage to forgive you, just this once."

Briar snorts again and takes another sip of her wine.

I guess I shouldn't be surprised that her eyes can no longer acknowledge other sexy men considering the fact that she's finally ditched the old asshat and found the man of her dreams. Now that she's all swoony in love, even managing to get her to take a *look* at Sexy Buns Guy should be considered a success in and of itself. Now, she only has eyes for one man.

"What did I miss?"

Speak of the devil.

Andy Marshall sidles up to our table, setting his second beer of the night on a cardboard coaster and slipping an arm around Briar's shoulders.

"Abby's making me stare at other men," she tells him, a faux pout on her face. Then she leans into him. "We're rating butts."

"Butt," I clarify, emphasizing the last letter and holding up my pointer finger. "One. One butt."

Andy hums, narrowing his eyes playfully before leaning forward. Briar and I follow his lead so we're all huddled close.

"Which one?" he whispers.

Briar lets out a long string of uncharacteristic giggles, which means the glass of wine she's been sipping on for the past while is finally beginning to have an effect. She points at where we've been looking.

Andy hums again, as if he's really considering his score. Then he turns his head to me, a serious expression on his face. "That's a five-star ass if I've ever seen one."

Briar's giggling increases, and I fall in with her, unable to help myself in the wake of Andy's incredibly accurate but also very funny assessment.

"Thank you," I say, turning to glare at Briar. "See?"

But she's too busy giggling and taking another sip from her quickly disappearing glass of wine. Someone's sure to have a rough hangover in the morning.

"So how's the packing coming?" Andy asks. "Did you actually end up starting, or will it be a mad dash after Christmas?"

"Maybe a little of both," I say honestly, wishing I could just snap my fingers and have all my stuff appear at the new place. "I'm actually a bit surprised by how much crap I have, so I've mostly just been throwing things away instead of packing."

I might be getting the larger room in the little two-bedroom house Briar and I are moving into at the start of the new year, but it's still a *little* two-bedroom house. It's unrealistic for me to think I can keep everything I've amassed in my twenty-four years of life.

In just a few short weeks, I'm finally moving out of my

brother Rusty's house, the childhood home where we both grew up. It's bittersweet, for both of us, and I think he might be taking it harder than he's letting on. Still, we both know it's time.

My brother is only six years older than me, and he's been forced to serve as a pseudo-parent for far too long. That's just one of the things that happens when you lose both of your parents before you become an adult. Well, Rusty was an adult at the time, but I definitely wasn't, and it meant he became the person I relied on for everything.

Eventually I moved away from Cedar Point to go to college, and each of us got a bit of freedom from each other. Some room to spread our wings. But when I decided to move back to town after graduating two years ago, I had no idea just how difficult it would be to live together again.

It has kind of cramped my style.

When I was in school, I was able to do what I wanted, when I wanted, without worrying what anyone else thought of me. Being back in my hometown, though, means I've had to put my good-girl hat on. I'm a little jealous of the fact that my brother doesn't seem to care *at all* what people here think about him.

I, on the other hand, am constantly concerned with how Cedar Point residents see the Fullers. There are only two of us left, after all, and my brother certainly isn't doing the family name any favors with his rough-and-tumble attitude and propensity for hooking up with women who aren't entirely available. Which means it's up to me to keep us from being the main subject of town gossip.

Just for a night, though, I'd love to take that good-girl hat and chuck it in the bin. Get back to some of the fun I had when I was in college, some of the freedom to go out and drink and hook up and do whatever feels right.

My attention shifts when I hear a metallic slap on the table and catch sight of a large hand as it's pulling back. I follow the movement until my eyes land on a man standing right next to me.

It's...

Holy shit, it's the guy from the bar.

The five-star-ass guy.

And damn if he doesn't look even better from the front than he did from the back.

"Let me know if you wanna use that later," he says, a smirk stretching across his face.

I'm stunned speechless, which is a miracle in and of itself, and I take a long, *long* second to peruse the man before me.

Thick brows. Deep-set steel-blue eyes that sparkle with humor. Honey skin that hints of time spent outdoors. A chiseled jaw covered in just the right amount of scruff. And a dark twist of a tattoo peeking up the side of his neck from under the thick flannel shirt he's wearing.

Before I can think to say anything in response, he winks and walks off, disappearing into the growing crowd.

I blink twice, fairly certain I just hallucinated the entire interaction.

But when I look down at the table, I know our brief encounter was very real. Because there, sitting in front of me, is a shiny silver quarter.

My eyes wide, I turn to look at my friends and find them both watching me in various stages of amusement. Briar's eyes are bright, her hand over her mouth in surprise. Andy is trying to hide his laughter behind his pint of beer.

"Was I really that loud?"

Andy snorts. "Well, *I* could hear your ass talk at the other end of the bar, so my guess is *he* could too."

I cover my face with my hand, the embarrassment washing over me as I realize my loud mouth has gotten me into trouble again. It's the one thing about me I can't seem to control.

I can work hard. I can be nice. I can volunteer. I can join in. I can be everything to everyone in any situation.

But the one thing I can't seem to control is my damn mouth.

"Well, are you gonna go after him or what?"

My head flies up, and I look at Briar in shock. "Excuse me?"

She just shrugs, as if she hasn't completely blown my mind.

"How many times have you told me you need to get laid?"

I glance at Andy and find his lips pinched together as he continues to fight his laughter.

Briar, oblivious to my embarrassment, continues. "Well, look where we are," she says, spreading her arms wide. "We are at the ultimate source of one-night stands. Time to take advantage, sister. Put up or shut up."

"Maybe we'll just"—Andy slips Briar's mostly empty wine glass out of her hand and scoots it across the table so it's out of her reach—"call it a night on the drinking, yeah?"

As Briar protests and Andy tries to convince her that one glass was enough, my eyes float around the room, considering what my best friend has said. Yes, she's slightly intoxicated. But she's also not at all wrong.

We've talked numerous times over the past few months since she's been home about the fact that I am in desperate need of some sexy fun in my life. It has been over two years since I've climbed into bed with anyone, and that was back when I spent every weekday on a college campus and had access to hot guys galore. The pool of available men in Cedar Point is a bit less crowded, and nobody has caught my eye since I moved back.

The bar we're in right now, Dock 7, is known for being the place to go if you're looking for some no-strings-attached fun and the hotspot for people in town on vacation. It's why the locals call the place Lucky's, and since it's the week before Christmas, the restaurant-slash-bar is packed to the gills with locals and visitors alike hoping to grab a drink, take a break from too much family time, and possibly find a ho, ho, ho.

Okay, that's kind of unfair, even if it *is* clever.

I purse my lips, my eyes looking off in the direction the mystery guy went, and then I look down at the quarter he left behind.

It was a sexy *and* funny way to get my attention, and I'm a sucker for a guy with a sense of humor. Maybe I should go find him. I am majorly overdue to have a little fun, and who better to have a steamy night with than some kind of mysterious stranger who's only passing through?

The longer I think about it, the more I realize I really do deserve it.

"Do you think he left?" I ask, my fingernails tapping along the side of my pint glass as my eyes continue to search the crowd.

"You're not serious."

I turn back to look at Andy, finding his expression stern and not at all as amused and playful as it was before.

"You don't know the guy," he adds. "It could be dangerous."

I tilt my head and pin him with a glare. "Have you ever had a one-night stand before?"

Andy's cheeks go pink, surely thinking back to the nights, years ago, way before Briar, when he and my brother would come here together looking for some of their own fun.

"That's different."

"Why? Because you're big and bad and can protect yourself?"

Briar pipes up. "That's sexist."

"Thank you, friend. It *is* sexist."

Andy lifts his hands in the air, clearly not wanting to be subjected to any more comments like that one. "Fine. I'll be quiet about it. Excuse me for worrying that you're going to go off and get murdered."

"The only thing that will be getting murdered is her vagina."

I slap a palm over my face at Briar's remark.

"Okay, I could have lived without *that*," Andy says, shaking his head and taking a long gulp from his beer.

Scooting around the table, I loop my arm into his. "Thanks for caring," I tell him.

Andy has been friends with Rusty for a long time. He's kind of like family, I guess, so it makes sense that he'd want me to be safe. But on a night I'm hoping to break some rules, a brother type is the last thing I need.

"And no telling Rusty," I add.

"Trust me," he says, pinning me with a look of his own. "I have absolutely zero interest in talking about this with your brother."

I grin, my eyes returning to scan the area in search of the mystery guy. Thankfully, I don't have to look for too long, because the crowd starts to shift and part at what seems like the exact right moment.

There he is, on the other side of the bar. Standing at another high-top table. Alone.

"All right, lovebirds," I say, tucking my hair behind my ears and hopping off my stool. "Wish me luck and a night of fun."

"Be safe," Andy says. "Text Briar a picture of his license if you leave with him."

"And his penis if you see it," Briar adds, a big smile on her face and her eyes glassy as she leans into Andy.

"Yeah, good luck with her tonight," I tell him. "She gets feisty when she drinks."

"I've noticed," he says, amusement coloring his voice.

Giving my friends a quick wave, I pick up the quarter and head off into the crowd, skirting around throngs of people to get to the other side of the room.

When I finally make it over there, I see the man of the hour leaning forward, his hands on his glass of beer as he twists it back and forth on the table between flat palms. Before I even have another second to think through what I want to say, he looks up, his eyes colliding with mine.

I register his surprise first, though it flickers across his face for only a second before that delicious smile from earlier returns. Just that look alone propels me forward until I'm across the table from him.

I take the quarter and set it down next to his glass, making the same loud *slap* noise he made when he set it down in front of me just a short while ago.

And then I say the most flirtatious thing I can manage to come up with, officially setting my good-girl hat on the shelf for the evening.

"I'm here to collect, if you're in for a little fun."

chapter two
abby

Confident. Sexy. Playful.

That's the vibe I want to give off to the tall stranger I'm hoping to leave with tonight. My efforts feel somewhat stiff, but he doesn't seem to notice if the way his eyes drop and give me a once-over is anything to go by.

They scan me from top to bottom. From the little black boots that pop me up a few extra inches, over my tight skinny jeans and long-sleeved wrap top, and then finally back to my eyes. I'm thankful I put a bit of extra effort into my look tonight, my long hair falling in loose waves in a way I know frames my heart-shaped face just right.

His entire perusal only takes a few seconds, but it sure does feel like it happens in slow motion on this end.

"That's cute," he says, eyeing me with unrestrained interest. "Can I buy you a drink?"

I shake my head. "Thanks, but I already had one tonight."

He watches me, his eyes sharp and attentive. "And one's

your limit?"

"It is if I'm planning to go home with someone." I give him my own up and down to fully take everything in. Dark boots, gray pants, blue sweater. Simple, classy, and damn sexy. "Gotta keep my wits about me."

His eyes drop to the table, and I catch him biting his lip as he picks up the quarter I set in front of him, tapping it against the wood a few times before returning those beautiful blues to me.

He's beyond attractive in a way they just don't make 'em around here, with a suave kind of sureness that can only come from a lifetime of getting exactly what he wants. Does it make me crazy to say I'm fairly confident he could ask me for practically anything and I'd give it to him?

Maybe.

But I'm trying to break the rules tonight, so being kind of crazy is certainly acceptable. Encouraged, even.

"You from around here?" he asks.

I nod. "Born and raised, which is why I know you're *not* from around here."

"That would be correct."

God, just talking to him is its own aphrodisiac. The man has one of those dimples in the side of his cheek, and it flexes and disappears every time he smiles. And the way his voice vibrates, hitting just the right timbre to send goose bumps skittering along the back of my neck and down my spine…is enough to make me want to throw caution to the wind.

"So, what brings you to Cedar Point?"

He lifts a shoulder. "A little bit of work, a little bit of play. Mostly just taking a breather from life."

I nod my head, understanding the sentiment. "Sometimes,

that's the best thing you can do," I tell him. "And Cedar Point is a great place to escape to."

Lifting a single eyebrow, he studies me. "Is it?"

"Definitely. Plenty of entertaining ways to spend your time."

We watch each other for a long moment, and that's when I catch him glancing down to my lips. It sends a surge of lust rushing through me, skittering along my skin and pooling in my stomach. That's the only explanation I can give for the words that come tumbling out of my mouth.

"Do you want to go somewhere?"

He gives me a look I can't quite describe, something that seems like surprise and desire and a bit of reserve all rolled into one.

"As in…"

It takes a second to realize he's trying to confirm what I mean.

"As in…back to wherever you're staying," I say, worrying I've misread this whole thing.

He's interested, right? I'm not confusing this, surely. It might have been a while since my last hookup, but I'm pretty sure I still know what blatant interest looks like, and this guy is showing it to me in spades.

"I'm at the resort tonight," he tells me, his eyes locking with mine as his fingers continue to rotate that quarter. "You wanna head there with me?"

Then he bites on his lower lip again, and it makes me want to yank him across this table to bite down on it myself.

"Definitely. If that's what you wanna do."

Finally, that smile of his makes a reappearance, and he takes a step closer to me, coming to the side of the table and slipping a hand down the length of my arm, a rush of goose bumps flooding in its wake.

"I can't imagine anything else I'd rather do with my night," he tells me.

And then he slips his fingers into mine and gives me a tug, leading me through the room and out of the bar.

The near-freezing air of nighttime in Cedar Point hits my face with a smack, but then I'm tucked in close next to a warm body as the two of us begin the short walk out to the parking lot.

I like the way my hand feels in his, encased in warmth and skin that's just slightly rough. I like the way he weaves us through the cars, glancing down at me once or twice with a look that sends nervous excitement skittering through me.

And I *really* like the way he turns me so my back is pressed against a fancy black SUV, his body coming in flush against mine.

"I've been wanting to do this since the second I saw you."

Then his lips are pressed against mine, our mouths opening and his tongue dipping in with that same confidence and surety that had me practically panting earlier.

God, this is a fucking *kiss*. A hot kiss filled with lust and desire and a hint of greed.

His body is thick and warm and muscular in all the right places, my hands roving and touching just about anything I feel brave enough to reach for.

He doesn't handle me with kid gloves, either, his hands dropping down along my waist and then back to grip my ass, before one hand firmly grips my thigh, tilting me just slightly so he's pressed up against me right...*there*.

I moan, somewhere deep in my soul, feeling the kind of devastating attraction I've only read about in books or heard about from my friends. I feel like a magnet, and he's my other half. I am powerless to want anything other than to be closer to him.

Which is why my mouth follows his when he pulls back, my brain in a lusty fog, unable to understand why the good stuff has suddenly stopped.

"Let's get going—otherwise I'm in danger of doing something indecent," he says, shifting us both to the side and opening the car door.

As he takes my hand to help me climb into the passenger seat, I smirk at him. "I'm hoping a lot of indecent things happen tonight."

The side of his mouth tips up. "You're a lot of trouble, aren't you?" he asks.

I wink and take my seat. "I guess you'll just have to find out."

He stares at me for a moment longer before he closes the door and rounds the front, and then he's climbing in on the driver's side and getting us on the road.

My entire body feels like it's vibrating, like the blood in my veins is pulsing and pounding, desperate for more of whatever kind of drug his kiss has introduced into my system. I remember random hookups when I was at school, and it *never* felt like this—like a fucking avalanche of sensation that can't be controlled or corralled in any way.

Looks like I just need to hold on or risk getting swept away.

It's only a few minutes from Lucky's to South Bank Resort and Marina, the one hotel in Cedar Point, and my escort makes quick work of parking and getting us inside. Then through the lobby, into the elevator, up to the third floor, and down a long hallway.

As soon as the door closes behind us and we're shrouded in the darkness of his room, we're reaching for each other. My arms wrap around his neck and pull his mouth down to mine. His hands grip my ass and lift me up so I'm circling his waist with my legs. Then I'm pressed against the wall, his body snug against mine as we kiss for long moments, our mouths dueling, eager, needy.

That's how he makes me feel. Needy. Like nothing I touch is enough. I just want more.

More. More. More.

Eventually he pulls me off the wall and carries me through the room, lowering me down so I'm sitting in front of him on the bed. Unable to help myself, my hands slip under his sweater and shirt to slide along the warm skin underneath, enjoying the feeling of the hard planes of his body. I've never been with anyone as big and muscular as he is. I may have joked in my mind earlier about him throwing me over his shoulder, but that fantasy isn't a joke—and I think this is the guy to make it a reality.

He shifts, stripping his shirt and sweater off, and just like that, my mouth goes dry. The light in here is minimal, mostly just coming from the moon outside through the window, but damn if I am not impressed by everything my eyes can see.

"You are so gorgeous," I say.

He steps into me, his own hands dropping down to tug at my top, his fingers moving slowly and sparking little fireworks as they brush along my skin.

"The feeling is one hundred percent mutual," he replies as I untie the bow at my hip to release my wraparound top.

His eyes move quickly across every newly exposed piece of skin, like he's trying to drink it all in. Then he's pushing me back on the mattress and climbing over me and slanting his mouth against mine.

Suddenly it feels like everything is happening with urgency, as if we can't get ourselves naked fast enough. I'm tugging off my jeans and he's unbuttoning his belt, trying to get his off as well. We're yanking at our own clothes and each other's, all the while kissing and touching and grabbing.

Somehow, he manages to strip first, and before I can take off my panties, his hand is slipping beneath the fabric, the movement enough to freeze me in place. We both moan when one of his fingers slides through the wetness between my legs, my head falling back against the mattress at the delicious sensation.

He watches my eyes, his own heavy-lidded, his mouth open slightly as he strokes between my lips, as my breathing begins to pick up at the feel of his rough fingers between my thighs.

"What's your name?" I pant, realizing I never asked.

"Jackson."

I moan. "I like that name."

"Yeah?"

Nodding, I decide to test it out. "Jackson," I say, licking my lips. "Fuck, that feels so good."

He groans, dipping his head and sucking on my neck. "It sounds good when you say it like that."

"Like what?"

"Like a prayer."

Then he takes that finger and slips it into me, watching with longing as I writhe beneath him.

"Like it's the most important word in the world."

His mouth returns to mine, nipping and biting at my lips before licking between them, his finger continuing to stroke in and out. In and out, his pace slow and steady, in no hurry.

It's so at odds with the way things feel inside me, with the way my body is squirming in need. I am desperate for him. For his body, for his mouth, for him to stroke on that spot he slides against when he touches me so deeply.

My eyes want to close as he brings me closer and closer to the peak, but I force them open, loving the way he's so focused on me. I'm lost in those steel blues that captured me from the first moment.

His head drops, his mouth closing over one of my nipples, alternating between licking and sucking as his finger strokes along something inside me that has my hips lifting up, my head flying back, my voice crying out his name.

"Jackson," I say. "Yes, right there."

And then I tumble over, ecstasy flooding through me in long waves that ripple through my entire body. Behind my ears, along my back, through my arms and out to my fingers and toes. It's delicious, and everything I've always believed an orgasm *could* be but have never experienced.

I'm barely starting to come down when I see him getting out of bed to cross the room…when I register the curse that falls from his lips.

"What's wrong?"

"I don't have a condom."

I finally look in his direction and find him standing with his pants in one hand and his wallet in the other, his jaw clenched with frustration.

"You don't have anything, do you?" he asks.

I shake my head. It's never occurred to me to carry condoms before, though I now realize how stupid that is.

He shifts where he stands, and that's when my attention drops to the hard shaft between his legs. When I look back up into his eyes, I give him my own smirk. We might not be able to get down to business, but that doesn't mean I can't think of a few different ways to take care of him. Ways I can make him squirm and moan, make him just as needy as he made me feel moments ago.

Jackson watches me as I shift my panties back into place and crawl to the end of the bed. Then I cross the room and take his hand in mine, tugging him over to the fancy arm chair that sits in the corner and pushing him into the seat.

"Just because we don't have a condom," I tell him as I twist my hair into a knot at the base of my neck, "doesn't mean the fun has to stop."

The hazy look of lust in his eyes and the way he reaches out to grip the armrests tells me he's exactly where I want him to be. Desperate. Hungry. Greedy.

I drop to my knees, using my hands to stroke along the skin of his thighs and hips, along that area right beneath his belly button.

And then I watch him as I take the flat of my tongue and stroke long and hard along the length of him, loving the way his mouth falls open and his eyes glaze over. He looks drunk on this, from just that one little tease.

He has no idea what he's in for.

I continue working him over for long minutes, until I can feel him trembling beneath my fingers, until he's so bristling with need that he digs his hands into my hair, tugging it free from the haphazard knot I attempted.

I open wide and take him in deep, encasing him in the wet heat of my mouth and letting him bump the back of my throat before I suck and slide along his length.

"Fuck," he says, dragging out the word as his head falls back.

But his eyes return to watching me almost instantly, almost like he can't resist seeing me on my knees before him. He bites his lip and begins to shift his hips in his seat.

I moan around his dick, enjoying the sparks of pleasure I get from where his hands in my hair are beginning to guide me to what he needs. I want this to feel as amazing for him as his attention felt to me, which is why I never look away, never stop the strong suck and bob, never falter my rhythm.

It's why I bring my hand up to tug and play with his heavy sack, then take the root of him into my hand, stroking at the area my mouth can't reach.

"Your mouth…" he says, his touch getting a little rougher, his movements a little more erratic, his body beginning to throb with the beginning of his release. "I'm gonna come," he tells me, and then seconds later, I feel hot spurts against my tongue and the back of my throat.

He sits there for a long minute after he's done, his eyes glazed over and his breathing heavy. Then he's yanking me up off my feet and carrying me over to the bed, the two of us stretching out and snuggling up in the blankets as he presses his lips to mine.

chapter three
abby

"Something's weird about you today."

I glance over at Ruth, my boss, finding her leaning against the front counter with her arms crossed and her gaze intent on me. Instead of continuing to watch *her* as she watches *me*, I return my attention to the glass container I'm emptying, removing the items that didn't sell today.

"There's something weird about me every day," I reply playfully, tugging the tray of brownies, seven-layer bars, and chocolate chip cookies toward me and out of the cabinet, then crossing to the back counter to begin wrapping them for tomorrow's discount basket.

"No, this is different," she insists. "You're like...even more cheerful, if that's possible."

I snort. "Thanks?"

"I'll figure it out at some point," she declares, winking and throwing me a smile before pushing on into the back of the store.

Once she's gone, I let out a long, slow breath, glad she didn't choose to prod me any further. I'm really good at keeping other people's secrets but *horrible* at keeping my own.

And I am bursting at the seams to tell somebody about what happened between Jackson and me last night.

I hum quietly as my mind replays the sexiest little something I've ever had in my entire life for at least the thousandth time today. Jesus, no wonder Ruth picked up on my weirdness. I've been a blissed-out zombie all morning, bopping around in the back kitchen while preparing several dozen Christmas catering orders.

Last night really couldn't have been any better. Sure, I could lament the fact that Jackson didn't have a condom, and maybe I'll wish for the rest of my life that we'd been able to actually get the full experience, because I bet sex with that man is insane. But damn if what we did together wasn't still pretty spectacular.

And honestly, as someone who doesn't hook up often, it was probably better that he *didn't* have a condom. In a world where I'm hoping to take my good-girl hat off more often, it was a nice baby step rather than a full kerplunk into the pool.

The only thing I regret a bit was not leaving him my number when I slipped out of bed in the wee hours of the morning to get home and showered before my shift at Ruthie's.

Cedar Point is fairly tiny, with only around 2,500 residents during the off season, and it only takes about thirty minutes to drive around the entire town. So, it was easy to walk the ten minutes back to Lucky's to get my car and drive home. Cold, but easy.

Thankfully, Rusty is a heavy sleeper and wasn't woken by my return home at o'dark thirty. I was able to quietly move through the house without him being any the wiser. It's not that I need

21

his permission to be out with a guy, but seriously, the last thing I want is my brother to know I was hooking up with some random tourist at the hotel.

That might be *his* style, but I'm pretty sure it'd break his brain if he found something like that out about me. In my defense, I've *never* had to deal with the conversation of dating or boys with my brother in my entire life. Ever.

When I was in high school and actually old enough to date, I wasn't in the right headspace to think about the stupid boys I went to school with. I was too busy trying to recover from our family tragedy to even think about the immature shits who sat next to me in class.

Then, when I left for college, I had enough distance to do what I wanted without thinking about my brother at all. I dated a few guys but never seriously enough for them to come home with me for the holidays or meet my brother when he'd come visit. Everyone else was just a hookup, so *definitely* not something I would tell Rusty about.

So, even though it would be nice to be able to enjoy myself occasionally with a stud who's only in town temporarily, I'd rather keep those tidbits about my sex life as much of a secret as possible.

After wrapping up my shift at Ruthie's, the town bakery and the best place to work in the world, I make the short drive home. I stay in my parked car after I've pulled into the driveway, knowing I need to call Briar to share what happened.

And make sure she's surviving her inevitable hangover.

"What."

I laugh at the sound of her voice, gruff and unhappy, like my phone call is the most inconvenient thing to happen in her entire life.

"You alive over there, drunkaroo?"

She groans. "Barely."

"You had *one* glass of wine, Briar. *One.*"

"I am very aware."

Shaking my head, I tap the call over to speaker and set the phone on the dash.

"You either need to stop drinking wine or start working on your tolerance, girlfriend."

"What do you think I was doing last night?"

"Getting drunk," I reply. "You need to start drinking entire glasses of water with your wine, lady. Andy had to take your drink away."

She chuckles and then groans. "Yeah, I know." Then there's an elongated pause. "Although, I must have gotten drunker than I thought because I *think* I remember somebody heading off in search of a one-night stand."

I smile but don't say anything.

"Abby."

"Oh, are you talking to me?"

"Funny."

I flip down the visor, examining my face in the mirror. My freckles are fading a bit in the winter weather since I'm spending less time outdoors. It bums me out some, because I've always thought my freckles make me cute. And the green eyes. Apparently they're rare, but both Rusty and I got them from our mom.

Wiping a smudge of mascara from under my eye, I consider whether Jackson liked my freckles last night...if he even saw them as we moved from the dim lighting of the bar to the darkness of his hotel room. Then I roll my eyes and smack the visor back closed. It doesn't even matter.

"Time to spill the beans," I hear from the speaker. "I remember him having an amazing butt, though not much else."

"See, I knew you'd eventually agree with me."

"Abby."

"Okay, fine. Yes, I hooked up with him last night, a decision you completely supported, in case you don't remember. He's a tourist and like a full foot taller than me, and I've never orgasmed that hard in my entire life."

"That is quite the endorsement."

I snort. "Ten out of ten, would recommend."

"Really that good, huh?"

I hum my agreement. "I almost regretted not leaving my number for him when I snuck out of his room this morning, but then I realized it would have been stupid, you know? To leave it and then wait for him to call when I doubt he ever would."

"It was smart to leave without attachments," she tells me. "Especially if you're just interested in a little fun."

I nod, though I know she can't see me.

Briar's right, and so am I. Leaving my number would have put an expectation on things, and the point of last night was exactly what Briar said. *Have a little fun.*

She and I have had quite a few conversations about the importance of finding a guy to just enjoy for a while. It's a recommendation I've given to her more than a few times in her life and one that eventually led her to her relationship with Andy.

Being at least partially responsible for them ending up together makes it harder to admit that sometimes I have a difficult time following my own advice. Even though what I *said* I wanted was some casual fun, I still have trouble separating the physical from the emotional. So, maybe what I *actually* meant was that I wanted something fun that could turn into something more.

I shake that thought off, trying not to dwell on it too much.

Maybe someday what happened for Briar will happen for me. Last night wasn't it, but that doesn't mean it can't happen in the future. That I won't find my own *someday* with the right man.

We shoot the shit for a bit longer, each of us promising to connect soon about our furniture situation for the new place—which is looking bleak as hell—and then we get off the phone, Briar likely curling back into a ball at Andy's to nurse her hangover as I head inside and try not to daydream about the man from last night.

I grab my purse off the passenger seat of my old blue VW Bug, climb out, and lock up before taking the path around the side of our house to the front door.

My mom put the stones in for the little walkway back when I was in junior high. The stones and all the little pink flowers that used to line the path. When she and my dad passed away at the start of my sophomore year of high school, I didn't know anything about taking care of plants or maintaining the outside of a house. Neither did Rusty. When those flowers suddenly died, having been scorched by the sun after not being watered, I was devastated.

Then one day when I came home from school, there were all new flowers lining the walkway. Rusty had gone down the mountain to one of those massive hardware stores that have a garden department, bought hundreds of dollars' worth of flowers, and replanted them along the edges. Yellow this time. Mom's favorite color.

Right now, there are just empty brown patches where the flowers used to be because the temperature is so dang cold, but they'll be back in a few months. After Christmas, after the yearly snow in January and February, the temps will start to warm up around mid-March, and that's when the flowers will be back.

Bright and sunny and yellow.

Although, I guess this year, I won't be living here to see them bloom.

As excited as I am to move, that thought has my heart dipping a bit as I walk through the front door. I may have moved away for college, but this has always been my home. Moving in with Briar on the other side of the lake changes that in ways I'm probably going to be learning to adjust to for quite a while.

"Hey, Rus," I say, rounding the corner from the entry.

My brother looks up from where he's bent over a bunch of papers spread out across the kitchen island. "Hey, Abs. How was work?"

"Good. Lots of tips today."

Dropping my purse at the foot of the couch, I shrug out of my jacket and walk over to hang it in the small closet off to the side of the six-foot Christmas tree we put up together last weekend. Then I crawl up onto one of the stools at the counter and reach over to the bowl of peanut M&M's sitting out.

As I stuff a few in my mouth, I register the unfamiliar phone on the counter, along with the notepad and pen resting in front of the other bar stool.

Then I hear the downstairs toilet flush.

My eyes narrow at my brother. "It's the middle of the day, Rusty," I say. "You couldn't have hooked up somewhere else?"

My brother's brow furrows like he doesn't know what I'm talking about.

"We talked about this. You promised you'd give it a break for a few weeks around the holidays until after I move out. We only have a little bit of time left with me living here, and I'd really rather there *not* be a string of women coming and going."

At that, I watch his forehead smooth out. "Oh, I don't have

a girl here," he says. "Remember I told you a buddy of mine was coming to town to help with some of the brewery stuff?"

I nod slowly, thinking back to a random conversation we had a month or so ago about a friend of his from college. Now I can't remember what was said.

"Kind of."

"Jackson's kind of a guru with launching small businesses, so he's going to help with—"

"Wait, wait," I say, blinking a few times and feeling like I might have just had a stroke.

There is *no way* I just heard that name come out of my brother's mouth.

"What did you say his name is?"

Rusty opens his mouth, but then his eyes shift to something behind me and he smiles.

"Hey, man. I want you to meet my sister."

I stay seated in my chair, facing my brother, saying a desperate little prayer that what I think is about to happen is not happening. Praying I misheard. Or misunderstood. Or that Jackson is suddenly a super common name in the world.

But of course that's not what happens at all.

When I finally turn around, I'm met with the same beautiful blue eyes that gazed into mine with lust and need and adoration as I knelt before him last night.

"Abby, this is my friend Jackson. Jackson, this is my sister, Abby," my brother says, coming around the island to wrap his arm around my shoulder, completely unaware of the fact that my stomach has launched itself into my throat.

Jackson stands there for a long moment, his hands tucked into the pockets of his jeans, his face decidedly blank.

"Nice to meet you," he says, that same sexy voice rumbling

through me just like it did as he pinned me up against his car.

"You, too," I manage to choke out, though just barely.

Because *what the fuck?*

"He's going to be staying with us for a few weeks," my brother says, completely oblivious to the fact I'm having an internal meltdown. "I was thinking we could take Jackson to The Mitch tonight. You know, give him a real local experience."

Jackson emits some kind of strangled laugh, and all I can manage is a wince, thankful that my brother isn't aware of just how much of a *local experience* his friend got last night.

Swallowing uncomfortably, I slip off my stool, suddenly desperate to be anywhere but right here.

"Why don't you two just go," I tell my brother. "I'm pretty tired. Long day at work."

Rusty gives me a look. "Since when do you turn down a free drink?" he asks. "Besides, Jackson's only going to be in town for a short time, and we've talked about you a lot over the years. I'm sure he'd love a chance to get to know you."

Somehow I manage to nod my head, though I know I'm going to keep scrambling for any kind of excuse to get out of grabbing drinks with my brother and the guy who had his dick in my mouth less than twenty-four hours ago.

"I need to shower off the day," I say, my voice coming out in an awkward squeak. Clearing my throat, I make a hasty retreat toward the stairs. "I'll see you guys…later. I guess."

And then I'm fleeing out of the room and up to my bedroom, wondering what the ever-loving hell is happening.

chapter four
jackson

I try not to stare for too long in Abby's wake as she hightails it out of the living room and upstairs, but it's difficult not to look in that direction and wonder what's going through her mind right now.

Because I'm fairly certain she was no more aware of this being the direction the day would take than I was.

"I don't know what's up with Abby, but I guess I shouldn't be surprised," Rusty says, humor in his voice. "I've always told you she marches to the beat of her own drum."

I nod, trying to push an easygoing smile onto my face.

"You said earlier that you forgot to tell her I was staying with you guys," I say, hoping to play down her reaction to me being in her house. "That's probably all it was."

My friend chucks a few M&M's into his mouth and bobs his head. "Well, regardless, I'm sure we'll be able to convince her to come with us tonight. She's the most important person in my life, and I want you to get to know her."

A prickle of unease settles along the back of my neck.

For as long as I've known Rusty, he's been a protective kind of guy, always looking out for others. He was that way when we met freshman year, and that part of his persona only intensified once his parents died and he left school a year early to come home and take care of his sister.

He used to tell me that in some ways, he's been more like a father to her than a brother with the kind of role he's had to take on in her life. How the hell am I supposed to live with the fact that I spent last night with my mouth all over her body and my fingers inside her?

Clearing my throat, I have to work not to get hard at just the memory, at the thought of what she looked like on her knees, her big green eyes looking up at me like I was a fucking king… what she looked like as she tossed her head back in pleasure while I brought her to an orgasm that nearly set me off as well…

Fuck.

"I'm gonna head to the store to grab some burgers to throw on the grill tonight. You wanna come with or stay here?"

The sound of Rusty's voice as I'm thinking about his sister is jarring, but I manage to respond.

"I think I'll stay here," I tell him. "Still a bit tired from the drive yesterday."

He nods. "Sure thing. Feel free to take a nap or something. We can eat whenever and swing by The Mitch later."

"Thanks."

Rusty grabs his keys and wallet off a small table in the corner, then gives me a wave before heading out the door.

I stand there for a long minute, my hands on my hips, looking around the room after he leaves. It looks different now with all the Christmas decorations and the tree and the two stockings hanging on the fireplace, but I've been in this house before. Once when we were still in college, before their parents died, and once a few years ago.

I can't help but wonder how in the *hell* I didn't realize that was Rusty's sister last night.

Crossing the room, I pick up a framed photo sitting on the mantel behind a string of garland. Two proud parents. Rusty. And Abby, still in braces and her hair in two French braid pigtails with little bows on the ends.

I set that one down and look at the next. This one I've seen before. It's Rusty and Abby at her college graduation. He sent it to me a few days afterward, telling me how proud he was.

How the fuck did I not make the connection?

How did I not recognize her from this picture?

Better yet, how did I never ask her for her name?

Abby.

If I'd just asked for her name, I would have known. Surely, I would have put two and two together.

But I didn't ask. I didn't *think* to ask. *Couldn't* think at all. I was too overwhelmed by how turned on I was by her cute pick-up lines and then the way it felt to kiss her. One thing led to another, and I could barely think straight.

I've never had a girl pick me up like that before. Normally, that's my job. And damn if it wasn't one of the hottest things I've ever experienced.

Both the picking up part *and* the time in my hotel room.

Fuck.

This morning, I woke up to an empty bed and the startling realization that I was disappointed to be alone. A quick look around the room confirmed the mystery girl had gone, taking all her belongings and sassy attitude with her and not leaving a note or anything behind.

I had quite a number of fun nights with women back in college, and I've gotten fairly familiar with the concept of *accidentally* leaving something behind. A bag. A brush. A hat. Something small and unimportant that requires a return trip to collect it, a chance to check in that doesn't involve waiting around on a phone call.

Girls used to do that all the time.

And yet this morning, the one time I actually *wanted* a girl—woman—to leave something behind so I could look forward to seeing her again, I was left disappointed.

Although, I guess it was for the best, right?

Rusty was there for me during one of the hardest times of my life—a true friend…family, if I'm honest. While I can't change the past, I can absolutely control myself in the future.

Even considering anything else with Abby would be flying in the face of the friendship I claim is so important. So I come to a decision that I know is ultimately right, even if it feels like someone is popping all my balloons.

Taking the stairs two at a time, I move quickly up to the second floor and down the hallway, passing the room on the left where we put my suitcases earlier and Rusty's room on the right, coming to a stop in front of the closed door at the end that can only belong to one person.

I breathe in deep, let it out slow, and then knock.

Only a few seconds pass before it opens wide, and Abby's standing in front of me in a pair of leggings and a loose tank top, one hand braced on the doorjamb and the other holding the door.

God, she's gorgeous.

She stares at me for a second before rising on her tiptoes and looking over my shoulder.

"Where's my brother?"

"He went to the store."

She nods, crossing her arms, her eyes assessing me. "I didn't know you were Rusty's friend, in case you were wondering."

"Yeah, I could…tell. Earlier."

What I want to ask is why she looked almost disgusted when she fled the room, but I keep that to myself. I don't want to know if finding out I'm her brother's friend changed last night for her, because it certainly doesn't change it for me—even though it probably should.

"So…you're staying here?" she asks, her eyes narrowing. "In the guestroom?"

I nod. "Yeah. Until after the new year."

"Why didn't you stay here last night?"

I nod, knowing this all might have been avoided if I'd just come straight here like I was supposed to.

"I originally booked a hotel, but Rusty practically demanded I stay with you guys. The resort wouldn't refund one of the nights, so I figured…why not? With the flight and the time change, I planned on grabbing a beer at the bar and then heading back to sleep."

And then I saw you.

There's a lull, where we just look at each other, and as much as I know I should be telling her nothing else can happen between us, something completely different comes out of my mouth.

"Why didn't you leave your number?"

It wasn't what I planned on asking, that's for sure, but it's the only thing on my mind at the moment. I can't imagine having a night like we did and then just…leaving.

33

Abby blushes, the apples of her cheeks tinging pink, and then that color moves through her face and down her neck.

I watch as she shifts on her feet a little, her eyes flitting all over the place—to my eyes, my arms, my feet, my mouth, my waist. It's like she doesn't know where to look.

"Last night was…" she starts, but her voice trails off.

"It was amazing," I say, unable to keep the thought to myself.

Her eyes finally connect with mine.

"It was the hottest thing I've ever experienced in my life," I continue, wanting her to know just how much I enjoyed it.

That pink in her cheeks grows, but I see her eyes drop to my mouth. Then she licks her lips.

I take a step toward her, crossing the threshold into her room. She doesn't step back. Just stands there, staring at my chest as I stop a few inches from her.

Unable to help myself, I lift a hand to her face, tucking her hair behind her ear and enjoying the way her entire body seems to shiver as her head leans into my hand.

"Abby," I say, loving the sound of her name on my lips, wanting her to look at me.

But she doesn't. She just keeps staring forward.

Which is why it's startling when her hand comes up to rest on where mine is cradling her face. Her eyes shut as her hand strokes along the back of mine, a single finger tracing up my forearm and bicep and then down to my wrist. It's a move that raises all the hairs on my body and has that familiar feeling of want and desire coursing through my veins.

I use my hand to tilt her head back and then bring my face close to hers so I can feel her warm breath on my mouth, so our lips graze each other's, our noses bumping.

God, I should be pushing away right now. Should be telling her nothing else can happen between us because Rusty is my friend…but damn if the desire racing through me isn't enough to keep me from making the right choice.

Ignoring my better judgment, I drop my mouth to hers, reveling in how quickly she opens for me, how desperately her tongue tangles with mine. It was like this last night too. Almost a desperate craving. An itch we both need to scratch. Like she was just waiting for me to make the first move.

Only a few blissful seconds go by before I hear the front door open and shut, followed by the sound of heavy feet walking through the house.

"Forgot my wallet!"

We stare at each other as we listen to Rusty moving around, and then there's the sound of the door opening and closing once more.

The minute he's gone, our mouths collide again, and I push my way into Abby's room, kicking her bedroom door closed.

Her tongue licks into my mouth with desperation, wiping away my earlier thought that something may have changed for her now that she knows I'm friends with her brother. She's just as hot for me as I am for her.

We're a tangle of limbs as we yank at each other, stripping from fully clothed down to nothing in the blink of an eye, slowed only by our need to touch each other at every second. I can't help but want to grip that ass and those hips as her sexy-as-sin body becomes bare to me.

"I still don't have anything," she tells me as her hand wraps around my dick.

I moan, unable to do anything but thrust into her grip.

"I went to the store this morning," I tell her, and when I

35

see her eyes widen, I smile. "You'll think I'm full of shit, but I was hoping to bump into you again, and I didn't want to be unprepared."

I watch as her lips tilt up at the sides in a smirk. "You sure it wasn't for all the other sexy girls in town?" she asks, continuing to stroke me as she rises up to suck on my neck.

Fuck, the way she touches me is unreal.

"Not a chance in hell," I tell her, and then I'm smacking her hand away and backing her up until she tips over onto her bed.

"Sorry it's a twin," she tells me.

"I'd fuck you on the floor if I needed to," I say, spreading her legs and looking down at the sweet heaven I hope to be lucky enough to get inside.

"I don't need foreplay today," she tells me. "I just want you inside me. Even if it hurts."

My eyes clamp shut and I groan. "*Fuck*. The things you say…" Then I let out a chuckle and reach over to my discarded pants to fish out my wallet. "You have no idea how damn hard you make me."

"Oh, I have a pretty good idea," she says, her eyes dropping down to watch me roll the condom on.

"So much fucking sass."

She grins and nods. "Always."

I step toward the bed, intending to climb between her legs, but she surprises me by moving around and telling me to sit on the edge so she can climb onto me.

"The whole time I was sucking you off last night, I kept thinking how hot it would be to ride you like this," she says as she straddles my hips and places her center at the head of my dick.

Then she leans in and puts her mouth to my ear.

"How deep you'd be able to go like this."

I grit my teeth, fighting off the first signs of orgasm at the base of my spine. The mouth on this woman is just...beyond me. Listening to her dirty-talking is unlike anything I've ever heard in my life, and it makes me feel like I could burst at any second.

She nibbles on my ear as she sinks down on me, slowly, whimpering the entire way.

All I can do is sit and accept it. If I move a muscle, she's going to be severely disappointed. My hands grip her waist, my fingers digging into her soft flesh as I try to control myself.

Once she's finally seated, she pulls back to look at me, and I love the way her pupils are blown, the dazed look in her eyes. I drop my hands to grip under her thighs and ass, and then I lift her up only to let her fall back down again.

She cries out, her head falling back, and I take a moment to appreciate one of the sexiest sights I've ever seen. Abby's pussy sucking me in, her tits bare and pointed and desperate, her head tossed back in ecstasy, her eyes closed. I take that mental image and store it for later, knowing I'm going to call back to this plenty of times in the future.

I lift her again and slam her back down, over and over again, pulling her close so I can lick and suck at her neck as she rides me.

"Jackson," she moans only a few minutes later. "Oh my God, I'm so close."

"Fuck yes. Come for me."

It's only a few more strokes inside her before she detonates, and I feel the sheer bliss of her inner walls clamping down on me with a force unlike I've ever experienced before. I call out her name, my hands gripping her tightly and holding her close as we both writhe through one of the hottest releases I've ever had.

We sit together like that for a long moment before she pulls back and kisses me. Hard and deep and filled with...something. Longing, maybe. Or maybe I'm just reading more into this than what's really there.

chapter five
abby

In retrospect, maybe I should have thought things through a bit more before agreeing to go to The Mitch with my brother and Jackson tonight.

In my defense, I'd just had one of the most explosive orgasms of my life. I was barely able to get in my shower and put clothes back on before Rusty was knocking on my bedroom door to tell me to get ready. In truth, my mind wasn't entirely in the right mental space to consider all the ramifications of such an outing.

Which is why I didn't think to ask if we were meeting anybody else there.

The Mitch is a townie dive bar about five minutes from our house, and I'm pleasantly surprised to see it isn't particularly busy when we walk into the dimly lit room. But as we cross through the haze, past the pool tables and the jukebox, to get to the table near the window that faces the lake, I realize there are two very familiar faces already seated and waiting.

"Hey guys," Andy says, giving us a wave as we approach.

As we all take our seats at the high-top table, I watch almost in slow motion as Briar gives Rusty and me a smile and wave as well…before her attention shifts to Jackson.

Briar's eyes squint, like she's trying to remember who he is, which makes sense since she was a little tipsy last night. Andy's eyes widen for a split second before he grins at me.

"You brought him!" he says, a jovial note in his voice.

There's brief pause where nobody says anything, and my mind scrambles to come up with just about anything I can possibly say in response.

"Did I tell you Jackson was coming to town?"

That question is from my brother, and Andy turns to look at him with stark confusion on his face.

"Jackson is my brother's best friend from college," I interject, trying to communicate to Andy and Briar with my eyebrows and widened eyes. "Apparently he's staying with us for a few weeks."

Andy's lips part like he wants to say something, but he stays quiet, his eyes flitting between all three of us.

"Yup. Helping me work on stuff for the bar," Rusty adds, slapping Jackson on the shoulder and giving him a grin, oblivious to Andy's bewilderment.

I'm not entirely sure whether Jackson recognizes Andy or Briar from last night, but I can tell he's picking up on the weird energy coming from my best friend and her boyfriend.

Jackson clears his throat and sticks his hand out. "Nice to meet you. What's your name?"

It takes a second, but Andy reaches out and shakes Jackson's hand. "I'm Andy Marshall. This is my girlfriend, Briar Mitchell."

"Haven't I seen you before?" Briar asks, her head tilted to the side as she continues trying to place him.

"I think we saw him at Lucky's last night, babe," Andy says.

"*Remember?*"

He looks at her hard, like he's willing her to remember that Jackson is the five-star ass.

Briar's eyes narrow and her nose wrinkles, but she just shakes her head. "No, I don't think it's that."

"Oh, that's right," my brother interjects, looking to Jackson and elbowing him playfully in the arm. "You mentioned that earlier." Then he looks at the rest of us at the table. "Apparently, Jackson found himself a local to have a bit of fun with last night."

My stomach dips and nausea builds as I have the sudden horrifying realization that Jackson talked to Rusty about what happened at Lucky's and the hotel. I glance at Jackson, heat building in my cheeks and neck as I search for some way to ask him what the hell he told my brother.

Logically, I can deduce the fact that they talked about it *without* the knowledge that I was Rusty's little sister, but still.

Ick.

"All I said was that I met someone last night," Jackson says to Rusty, though he glances at me. "I didn't go into detail."

The tension in my shoulders eases, just slightly. I was having visions of the two of them exchanging blow-by-blow stories, and that would probably ratchet up my nausea to the point that I'd be rushing to a bathroom stall.

"Psht. That's not all you said," my brother says, slapping Jackson lightly on the bicep before looking back at us. "Apparently, she was the most beautiful woman he's ever seen, and he wants help figuring out who she is because she snuck out this morning."

My lips part in surprise as my eyes dart to Jackson's, and what I find there confirms what Rusty said. He's looking down at the table, a few small flushed spots on his cheeks. He really was hoping to find me? That wasn't just a bullshit line earlier?

The nausea I was feeling before begins to dissipate at the realization, and something much warmer and more soothing takes its place as a smile tugs at my lips.

I'm not trying to delude myself with visions of grand gestures or anything crazy romantic happening between the two of us, especially if Jackson is just in town to help my brother with stuff related to the brewery-slash-taproom thing he's planning on opening. But I also can't help the swoop that happens in my belly at knowing he was just as into me as I was into him.

Suddenly, Briar gasps loudly, her eyes going wide as she looks between Jackson and me.

"Oh my God."

"You know, I don't think I need your help, actually," Jackson interjects, interrupting Briar before she can say anything else. "I mentioned it in passing, but it doesn't have to be a big deal."

"Nah, we've gotta help you find this girl," Rusty says, clapping his hands together and rubbing his palms back and forth. "If she's a local, one of us will definitely know her."

My eyes flit over to Briar's, finding her staring at me with wide eyes and a half-smile that makes her look constipated.

"She's not in here, is she?" Rusty asks, his eyes searching the room for any woman he thinks might fit whatever information Jackson gave him about her. About *me*.

"Uh…" Jackson trails off, looking incredibly uncomfortable. "Let's not do this, okay? It's really not that big a deal."

"Yeah, Rus. Just let it go if he doesn't want to talk about it," I say. "Besides, it could have been another tourist staying at the resort."

Rusty's head tilts back, like he didn't even hear me.

"Who do I know that was at Lucky's last night?" he says, one hand coming up to stroke his full beard. Then he looks back at Briar and Andy. "Did you guys see any…"

He pauses, and I see his eyes darting around the table before coming back to look at me.

"How did you know he was staying at the resort last night?"

There's a long pause where I realize I have two choices.

I can deny, deny, deny, and possibly avoid a conflict with my brother, making up some bullshit explanation about how *obviously he would have been staying at the resort, don't be an idiot.*

Or, I can just be honest with him about it.

Understandably, the last thing I want to do is tell my brother *anything* about my sex life, but we're always honest with each other, even when it's hard. I don't want to start lying to him now.

"Because it was me," I finally say, shrugging a shoulder and trying to play it off like it's the simplest, not-a-big-deal thing in the world. "I was the person he hooked up with last night."

I watch my brother blink a few times. And then continue blinking, almost like he's a robot that's short-circuiting.

"Let's go grab a drink," Andy says, tugging Briar away from the table with speed and efficiency I can't help but admire.

Their departure leaves just my brother, Jackson, and me at the table, along with a heaping ton of tension if the way Rusty is looking between the two of us is anything to go by.

For a brief moment, I wonder if he might let it go. If he might be a pseudo-parent instead of an angry big brother.

And then he speaks.

"You hooked up with my fucking sister?" Rusty hisses, glaring at his friend.

"I didn't know she was your sister last night," Jackson says.

"You expect me to believe that?"

"Yes, I do. I wouldn't lie to you. She didn't tell me her name."

I cringe, wishing *that* hadn't been shared. I can get over needing to come clean to my brother about the fact that we hooked up, but the things I do in my private life should still be somewhat private. Rusty doesn't need to know I went home with someone without exchanging names.

And of course, at that bit of information, his attention shifts to me.

"You went back to some random guy's hotel room and didn't even know each other's names?" he says, his eyes narrowed. "What kind of trashy shit is that?"

I pull my shoulders back and glare at my brother, surprised by the direction the conversation has taken.

"Excuse me, I don't think I heard you correctly," I say, sarcasm evident in nearly every bone and muscle in my body. "Did you just call me *trashy*?"

"Did you. Go home with someone. Without knowing his name?" His words come out in short chunks, his entire body bristling with irritation.

"Do you. Remember the name. Of the redhead from last week?"

Rusty's eyes narrow at me. "We're not talking about me," he says. "We're talking about my baby sister."

"And if your *baby sister* wants to go hook up with somebody, name or no name, you don't get to have an opinion."

"Fuck if I don't."

"Oh really? Mister brings-all-the-girls-home-all-the-time is gonna have an opinion on *me* hooking up?"

"It's different."

"Is it? Is it different?"

"Yes."

"Why? Because when you do it, it's all fun and fucking, but when *I* do it, it makes me a whore?"

My brother's expression shifts, something a little more like contrition hidden beneath his anger, but I'm too enraged to care.

"You are being the biggest hypocrite right now," I spit out, righteous indignation flooding my body. "If I were a guy, you'd be patting my back if I'd found someone hot to go home with last night. It wouldn't have even *occurred* to you that there was an issue with not knowing someone's name."

Rusty crosses his arms but stays silent. Smart man.

"The world we live in is filled with women who want different things, Rusty. Some women want to wait until they're married. Others want to fuck constantly and never get married. And then there are a million levels in between. Guess what is on *none* of those levels? Room for a man's disapproval. You wanna have opinions about shit? Be my guest, but keep them to your own damn self. I'll be over here, enjoying the choices *I* make, *without* consulting you."

Part of me wants to get up and storm out of the bar, but I know that's not fair to Jackson. I can't just leave him here to get reamed out by my brother. We hooked up *together*. We can deal with my brother's asshole-ish response together as well.

Rusty sits staring at me for a long minute before he turns to look at Jackson.

"And what do you have to say for yourself?"

Jackson shrugs a shoulder. "Is there anything I *can* say?" he asks. "It seems like you're going to be pissed no matter what."

Rusty looks from Jackson to me and then back to his friend.

"You swear you didn't know she was my sister?"

Jackson shakes his head. "I didn't know…" he says, pausing. I want to slap my hands over my face when he continues.

"…the first time."

Rusty's body goes rigid. "What?"

Jackson takes a deep breath. "We also hooked up earlier today," he says, glancing over at me before returning to focus on my brother. "You're my closest friend, Rusty. If you're upset about something, I need to be completely honest with you. I know how important the truth is to you, and that's the truth."

I bristle a bit, realizing the power dynamic has shifted. When Rusty first got upset about this, it felt like it was me and Jackson versus my brother. I thought he was on my side. Now, though, I'm realizing he's loyal to my brother first.

Which, I guess, isn't necessarily a bad thing. Rusty and I have had a lot of loss in our lives, parents and friends alike. If he and Jackson are as close as it sounds like they are, the last thing I want is for something to come between the two of them.

Rolling my eyes, I decide to add my own two cents.

"Look, Rus, it was just a little lust, okay? We hooked up last night and then today. It's out of our systems now. All right?"

I studiously ignore Jackson, focusing all my attention on the man who has spent his entire adult life sacrificing for me. Even though I'd love nothing more than to have a fun fling with the man sitting to my right, my undying love and loyalty is owed to the man on my left.

Rusty sits silent for a long moment, looking between the two of us with an unreadable expression on his face. Then he looks at Jackson.

"If you're here to invest in the brewery, you're here for the brewery, and that's it. Got it?"

Jackson doesn't say anything at first, and for a minute, I wonder if he's going to tell my brother no. Tell him he's too interested in me to promise nothing will happen between us.

And I'm honestly startled by how much I enjoy the thought.

But then I see Jackson nod in my peripheral vision.

"Got it."

"Let's just...pretend none of this happened," Rusty says, picking up his half-empty beer and downing the rest in one go.

I glance over at Jackson just for a second and find him looking at me as well.

Sure. Pretend it never happened.

Easier said than done.

chapter six
Jackson

When Rusty and I were in college, he bailed me out of a pretty shit situation that pretty much solidified our friendship.

We were freshman roommates and had grown to be pretty close friends when I decided to join a fraternity. Pledging takes up a shit ton of time, and it didn't take long for my social life to get booked up by my new brothers. Then I moved into the house sophomore year instead of getting an apartment with Rusty, like we'd talked about doing. Life went on for both of us, and it felt like we grew apart.

Halfway through the semester, in an incredibly stupid moment, I took some pills given to me by a fraternity brother at a party and ended up in the hospital. My so-called brothers didn't want to come get me because of the risk of getting into trouble or getting pinned as the person who gave me the drugs.

It was Rusty who came to pick me up. He walked in and talked to the doctor, made sure to get a full rundown of my health and anything I needed to do when I got home. Then he told me to come stay on his couch for a few days until I was feeling back to rights.

He's just always been that guy. The protector. The father figure, even though we're the same age. I've never been that close with my parents, so Rusty's care and concern, the way he looked out for me...it's always stuck with me.

Which is why it was totally unsurprising that he withdrew from school during the first week of his senior year to move home and take care of his sister. His parents were killed in a drunk driving accident, and at barely twenty-two, in the midst of his own grief, he became Abby's guardian. Left his entire life and future behind, dropped it all like a sack of bricks to be there for her.

I've always wished there had been something I could have done back then, some way I could have been helpful and supportive. But when you're just a college kid, and a friend is dealing with a tragedy like the one he and Abby were facing, it feels like there's absolutely nothing in the world you can do to make any difference.

Now that Rusty and I are a lot older—thirty-one and thirty-two, respectively—I feel like this brewery pub is a way for me to finally be able to support my friend. A way for me to repay him for the times when he's sacrificed for the people he cares about. Though he would kill me if he ever heard something like that come out of my mouth.

He has a pretty fantastic vision for his company, Cedar Cider, which currently operates as bottled beer that gets shipped out to retailers. In a small town like Cedar Point, which has so few options for drinks and dining, there is absolutely enough demand to open up an establishment like the one he is hoping to get going this year.

All he needs is some additional investment.

Apparently, a friend he grew up with here in town is one of the other investors, but he just wants to provide the financial capital and not be involved in the decision-making because he lives on the other side of the country.

I'm more of a hands-on kind of investor, which is the reason I'm here in town in the first place—to help Rusty scout locations, build up an operational business plan, and talk through some of the more important details. We might have both wanted to get our degree in business back in the day, but I was the one out of the two of us who was able to go on and finish.

Now I'm here to help, however I can.

If that includes staying away from his sister…I guess that's just how it is.

Last night was brutal, sitting across from Rusty and Abby as they fought, then having my friend's frustration turned and directed toward me.

I'm pretty sure I upset Abby by being so forthcoming with her brother, but it's important to me to be honest with him. I know, in some ways, he looks up to me, but there are plenty of ways that *I* look up to *him*. The last thing I want to do is let him down or make him think that I don't value our friendship.

Which is why I agreed to pretend my night—and the following day—with Abby never happened.

Even if actually forgetting about it is less likely than a fucking snowstorm in hell.

Maybe, *maybe* I would have been able to push things aside after our night in my hotel room, but after the sex in her bedroom? The way she sat astride me and whispered dirty things in my ear?

Fuck.

I might not jump into bed with as many women as I used to back in my college days, but I have racked up quite a few notches on my bedpost. Even so, yesterday afternoon in the bright light of day with Abby might have been the hottest thing I've ever experienced in my entire life.

So, yeah...I can *pretend* to forget what it felt like to have her wet pussy around my dick, but hell if I'm actually going to.

Even now, as Rusty and I wander through an old barn south of Main Street—our third stop of the day—I'm having a hard time getting her out of my thoughts. I lay in bed last night and jerked off to the memory of her whispering in my ear about sitting on my lap. *How deep you'd be able to go like this*, she said. I came faster than when I was a damn teenager.

Then this morning, when I went down to the living room for a bowl of cereal and found Abby sitting at the counter in her pajamas, I was more than a little irritated by the fact that I was turned on by the sight of her in a pair of sleep shorts and her feet in those fuzzy socks girls like to wear during the winter.

I had to retreat back upstairs to take a shower. A cold one.

I think it's safe to say that, as good as my intentions are when it comes to Rusty, I highly doubt his sister will be leaving my fantasies anytime soon.

"I think this is the one."

Spinning on my heel, I turn back to look at my friend, and I can't help but smile at the look on his face.

Rusty's never been a particularly boisterous kind of guy. Yes, he's friendly, and yes, the ladies would say he's charming—a trait he's able to pull out when it suits him. But he's actually more of a surly, quiet bear, which is why it's always interesting to see what will make him look like he does now.

Eyes bright with a small smile.

Usually, he only looks like that when he talks about his sister. It's that whole semi-dad, proud parent thing.

If that expression is on his face now, it means he's really excited about this place. With how thorough he's been on gathering information about properties before we visit them in person, I can't help but trust his judgment, especially since I've seen the spec sheet on this property. It really is a great fit for what he wants to do.

"Honestly, Rusty, I think this would be a great choice."

"You like it too?" he asks, his eyes still perusing the space, as if he hasn't already memorized everything.

I nod. "I do."

"There's plenty of room to build out a kitchen over here," he says, wandering over to one side of the room and opening his arms wide. "And there's a bunch of land out this door to build up the brewing facility and a parking lot. There's already plumbing installed. The structure is older but built to code."

"And it just looks fucking dope as shit," I add, knowing the truth.

That's when I get the full smile out of him.

"It does look pretty amazing, huh? Just needs some paint and a sign."

I nod. "And I bet it looks even better during the spring and summer."

The people that call Cedar Point home will definitely enjoy a little spot like what Rusty is dreaming up, but the customers who are going to absolutely flock here are the tourists that come to town during the high season. People like me. Twenties and thirties, and really into travel and collecting experiences. A local brewery with delicious grub and a social media friendly aesthetic? It's basically hipster heaven.

Rusty claps his hands together and looks around one more time. "Okay, then. Let's call Shawn with an offer."

The two of us head out to the car, and I drive while he calls the current owner of the barn to discuss terms of sale. It's somewhat unorthodox since they're not involving a realtor, but apparently that's pretty common in this town when properties exchange hands between residents.

Their conversation goes on for quite a while, lasting the entire drive back to Rusty's house. Once we arrive, he heads into his office and closes the door, leaving me to my own devices.

Which is how I find myself in the living room with Abby as she wraps Christmas presents at the kitchen island.

"Hey."

She glances over at me, then returns her attention to the task she's working on.

"Hi."

"You wrapping presents?"

"Yup."

I nod, heading into the kitchen, to the other side of the island.

"Who are they for?"

She takes a deep breath and lets it out long and slow.

"This wrapped one is for my brother. The coffee press is for Briar, and the *World's Worst Boss* mug is for Andy."

My brow furrows. "Is Andy your boss?"

"No, he's Briar's," she says, looking at me with a mischievous smile. "And according to this," she adds, holding up a to/from sticker, "that's who it's coming from."

I chuckle, putting a hand on the edge of the counter and leaning forward. "Clever. You know, when I was younger, I never—"

53

"You don't have to do this."

Abby's interruption surprises me, mostly because I have no idea what she's talking about.

"Do what?"

"Do...*this*. The small-talk thing."

I cross my arms, still feeling confused.

"I don't follow."

She sighs, setting the wrapped gift aside, then picks up the coffee press and places it in the center of the next sheet of wrapping paper.

"You feel awkward because we slept together, and your moral compass tells you you've betrayed my brother. You don't want to make *me* feel awkward by ignoring me while you're here, because...well, because we slept together and you probably have the somewhat misguided idea in your mind that every woman develops an emotional attachment to men they have sex with."

I watch with raised eyebrows as she quickly and efficiently wraps the box, realizing Abby sure does think she knows what's going on in my mind—though she could not be more wrong.

"So I'm just letting you know I *haven't* developed an emotional attachment to you, and you *don't* have to talk to me for fear that I'm going to feel neglected or something. That's what I mean when I say you don't have to do this. You don't have to pretend to want to talk to me. I would be just as happy sitting here alone."

She finishes wrapping the coffee press and puts a sticker on it in the corner, and then she looks up at me when I don't say anything.

I try to decide what I want to say to her and how. Honestly, the only thing running through my head right now is how much Rusty bragged about Abby being so fucking smart, and here she is, being exactly the opposite.

"Do you wanna know what I did last night?" I say, leaning closer to her and lowering my voice.

Her head tilts to the side and her eyes narrow.

"I jerked off in bed to the thought of your pussy clenching around me like a goddamn vise."

I can tell I've shocked her, because I watch Abby's eyes widen and can see her visibly struggle to swallow.

"And then this morning, when I came downstairs to get breakfast, you were sitting at the counter in those fuzzy socks… I could see your nipples through your shirt, and I had to go take a cold shower."

Her jaw drops, and if I'm not mistaken, something a lot like lust begins to cloud her eyes.

"You might think it's easy for me to just pretend the night at the hotel didn't happen or that yesterday we didn't fuck like rabbits in your childhood bedroom, but you couldn't be more wrong. All I want to do right now is yank you down off that stool and bend you over this island."

Abby blinks at me a few times, and I can see the way the red in her cheeks is rushing down and coloring her neck as well. She clears her throat. Then clears it again.

"I like you," I tell her, fisting my hands and resting them on the island, leaning close. "So *this*," I say, referring to the small talk, "has nothing to do with awkwardness and emotional attachment and everything to do with the fact that I'm at serious risk of doing exactly what I told your brother I *wouldn't* do."

Abby's lips tip up slightly at the edges. "Oh."

We watch each other, the only sound around us the ticking of the clock that rests on the mantel. She opens her mouth, just a smidge. But I hear the office door open behind her.

"We got it!"

Rusty's voice has me pushing back from the island, where I was hovering far too close to his sister. Abby reaches out and grabs the coffee mug, setting it on the next sheet of wrapping paper.

"We got it, Jackson."

I look up as Rusty enters the room, a smile on his face.

"Yeah?"

"Yeah."

"That's awesome. I'm so stoked for you."

"For us," he says, crossing into the kitchen and opening his arms to bring me in for a bear hug. "Stoked for *us*."

I hug him as well and pat him twice on the shoulder, feeling that same surge of guilt rushing through me as I look at Abby, literally behind his back.

Her eyes stay carefully down as she works on her wrapping.

And then I repeat his words.

"For us."

chapter seven
abby

"I have something special for you tomorrow."

I look up from the book I'm reading in bed and find Rusty standing at the door to my room.

"Oh yeah?"

He grins and nods. "Yeah. So don't sleep in too late, all right?"

"But what if I'm too tired to get up early?" I ask, stretching my arms above my head and giving him a super-wide smile.

I'm one of those weird people who doesn't like to get up early on Christmas, and this isn't just an adult trait. I was like this as a kid too. It used to drive Rusty insane because our parents would make him wait until I woke up naturally before we could open gifts.

Who am I kidding? It *still* drives him insane, because I *still* like to sleep in. Although, once our parents were gone, he took it upon himself to break the *wake up naturally* rule and began dragging me out of bed by eight.

"Set your alarm," he says, pinning me with a look. "Please."

I sigh. "Okay," I tell him, dragging out the word as if he's asking me to do something insane. "I guess I can do that."

He crosses the room and plants a kiss on my forehead, then turns to head out.

"Rusty?"

My brother turns back to look at me.

"I know sex stuff is probably the last thing you want to talk to me about, but I just want you to know…you don't always have to act like a dad, okay?"

He doesn't say anything, just watches me from where he stands in the doorway.

"You know I love you more than anything," I say, "but there are going to be things in my life that I do that you'll disagree with, and that has to be okay. I can't make every choice based on whether you approve or not."

Rusty's hands rest on his hips, his eyes studying me.

"I'm just protective of you," he finally says. "And the way Jackson slept around back in college…I wouldn't have let him anywhere near you back then."

"But that's not your decision to make," I say, trying to keep my voice soft. Nonconfrontational. "And even if mom and dad were here, it wouldn't be up to them, either." I pause, wanting to get this right. "I love you. You are the most important person to me on this earth. But I'm an adult, and it's important that I'm given the chance to make my own choices in life. Even if you think they're wrong. Because something that might be wrong for you might be right for me."

He stands there for another long moment before he bobs his head just once, seeming to take my opinions and words to heart. Then he turns toward the door.

"Night, Abs. Love you."

"Love you too."

He gives me a small smile and shuts my bedroom door, and then I hear him walk down the hall to his own room.

It's been a long time since I've had a conversation like that with my brother. Most of the time, I just go along with what he says. I might be a fairly opinionated person, but I'm also pretty easygoing, and it just makes life easier sometimes to not be a stick in the mud.

But this simply wasn't one of those things. With me moving out in just a week, it's going to be more and more important that I defend my right to make my own choices. Even if it makes things harder for my brother.

I flip off the light and climb into bed, hoping the glass of wine I had earlier will be enough to send me off to sleep quickly. The three of us spent Christmas Eve at Briar's parents' house, just like Rusty and I have done for every major holiday since my parents died, enjoying dinner and a little gift exchange.

There's always something magical about being in the Mitchell house for Christmas. Patty is the world's greatest host, and her home is always perfectly decorated and welcoming in the best of ways. It's what I aspire to have my future home be like when I have a family someday.

Briar is one of five siblings, and even though they don't all make it home every year, this is one of the years when every one of them is in Cedar Point for the holidays. With the Mitchell family, significant others, and a handful of neighbors and friends, it was quite a full house for dinner—and *quite* a rousing game of Cards Against Humanity.

Eventually, we all ended up sitting next to the fireplace and exchanging gifts—Briar loved the coffee press, and she and Andy had a good laugh about the mug—before Mark gave the three of us a ride home.

As much as I tried not to, as much as I tried to remind myself that he's my brother's friend and he wants to preserve their relationship, I couldn't help but glance at Jackson what felt like every few minutes all night long. I don't know what the hell that conversation was with him earlier today at the kitchen counter, but for some reason, it feels good knowing he's been just as wound up as I have.

Though I guess it doesn't matter since we're not going to do anything about it.

I lie in bed for what feels like hours, though when I glance at the clock on my phone, I groan in frustration to see it's barely after eleven. Instead of tossing and turning, unable to turn off my mind, I slip out of my bed, tug on a sweatshirt, and then move quietly through the house and down to the kitchen.

When I was a kid, decorating the tree with my mom was my favorite part about the holidays, and every year, we'd stay up late on Christmas Eve, drinking hot chocolate and watching the lights. In the spirit of that old tradition, I pull out some milk and sugar and a package of cocoa powder and get to work. It only takes a few minutes, and once I have my mug of chocolatey goodness, I plop in a few mini marshmallows and sit cross-legged on the carpet next to the tree, watching the twinkling lights as they flicker throughout the room.

I loved my parents a lot. I feel kind of stupid even thinking that, because of course I loved them. Losing them was the hardest thing I've been through in my entire life, and I'm so thankful I've had my brother to lean on over the years, to look to for support and guidance as I've grown older and faced different challenges and frustrations.

We may have had varying ideas about how to handle our grief—he likes to get rid of things that remind him of the life we used to have, and I like to cling on to my memories for dear life—but we're always here for each other. It's crazy to think about in the face of the tragedy we've been forced into, and we really are truly lucky to have the relationship that we do.

My head turns when I hear soft footsteps on the stairs, and I can't help the zing of pleasure that surges through me when I see Jackson emerge at the bottom. He's wearing a similar outfit to mine—a pair of plaid pajama bottoms, a hoodie, and some socks—and he heads my direction when he sees me sitting on the floor.

"Can't sleep?" I ask, my head tilting back so I can look at him as he towers over me.

He shakes his head. "Not a wink. You?"

"Same. There's hot chocolate on the stove if you want some."

Jackson smiles. "That actually sounds really good."

Heading into the kitchen, he makes quick work of preparing himself a mug, and then he crosses the room and lowers down to take a seat next to me.

"So, what are we doing?" he asks, blowing into his mug and looking up at the tree covered top to bottom in shiny bulbs and twinkling lights.

"Just enjoying some memories," I tell him. "Christmas is my favorite holiday, and it was my mom's too, so I always like to sit in front of the tree and think about her."

"I'm sorry about what happened to them. I know it was a long time ago, but I'm sure it's something you just don't ever really get over."

I nod, my eyes dropping to the mug in my hands.

"Yeah. Most of the time, life is just life. But then something will happen and I wish they were able to be there, or that I could have told them about it. I think those are the most difficult times. *Those* are the things it's hard to get over."

Jackson's silent for a long moment. "You know, I met your mom once."

Grinning, I turn away from the tree to look directly at him. "Really?"

He nods, his eyes focused on the lights twinkling along the walls and filling the room. "Yeah. I came here with Rusty once, just for a night. We came to town to pick up some of his stuff, and your mom was outside planting flowers."

At that, I can't help but smile. "She did love her garden."

"We only talked for a few minutes before she shooed us off to grab Rusty's things. But she seemed like…the kind of mom everyone wishes they had."

"She was," I tell him, knowing in my heart of hearts that it's true, that the world was robbed of my parents too soon.

"It's been a long time since I've had my own tree," Jackson says.

I appreciate the change in subject, knowing that memories about my parents are a double-edged sword. Wonderful things that can bring both a smile to my face and a tear to my eye.

So I latch on to what Jackson has said, shock etched in my voice. "Seriously?"

He nods.

"God, I can't imagine Christmas without a tree."

With a shrug, he sets his mug down on the carpet, then leans back on his palms.

"My parents and I aren't close, and they don't host holiday stuff like your friend's parents, so…" He shrugs again. "I usually just enjoy other people's trees."

the start of someday

One of my brows dips. "Is that what you do during the holidays, then? Visit friends?"

"For the most part," he says. "There are a lot of beautiful places to visit during December."

I nod. "I'm sure that's true. But there's nothing like being at home during the holidays. That kind of warm sense of…well, of *home*." Shaking my head, I grin, knowing that even with all the tragedy Rusty and I have faced, we're still lucky to have what we do. "It's special."

"I wouldn't mind having a place to spend every holiday," he says. "I'm not opposed to it. I just…haven't found anywhere that's made me think *this is where I want to be* yet."

"Well, if you're going to be spending the holidays somewhere this year, I'm glad it's with us," I say, giving him a grin. "It's important to be with people you love at the holidays, and it sounds like you and Rusty are close."

Jackson's lips tip up. "Yeah. Well, we *were*, for a long time. It's hard now, since we live so far apart."

"Where do you live?"

"Chicago."

"Oh, wow. That is far."

Jackson nods. "It is. And it's a lot colder during the winter."

"Do you like it there?"

He dips his head from side to side. "It's fine." Then he blows into his mug to cool his drink before taking a sip.

"Just fine?"

One side of his mouth curves. "I've been considering a change of scenery."

"Well, if you're investing in Rusty's brewery, you could always move here," I say. Then I freeze. "I mean, for the business," I clarify. "Not for like…any other reason."

Jackson pinches his lips together in amusement as he watches me stumble over myself. "Thanks for the tip."

I narrow my eyes at him. "That's my line."

"Oh I certainly gave you more than just the tip," he shoots back, one eyebrow rising high on his forehead.

His comment has me bursting into giggles, and I hide my face in my hands for a moment, trying to collect myself. Eventually, I manage to calm down, even though Jackson is still eyeing me with that little smidge of deviousness.

"You said you were remembering your mom when I came down," Jackson says, completely redirecting our conversation. "Tell me one of your favorite holiday memories of her."

I grin, my mind flitting back over years' worth of things that, at the time, seemed like they didn't matter.

"Okay, well…when I was in elementary school, my parents wanted us to go to this apple orchard up north. Rusty and I were so not into it, but my mom insisted, so we all bundled up and loaded into the car in the middle of November, just a week before Thanksgiving, to drive down the mountain, two hours north, and then up another mountain."

I giggle, shaking my head.

"Rusty and I were miserable, and we fought and complained the whole time. Then when we finally got there, it was crazy foggy. Like, my dad could barely see the road in front of him, and the orchard's restaurant and gift shop were open, but the apple picking wasn't. So we drove hours and hours to spend ten minutes at this place, where my mom finally just bought a sack of apples before we went home."

Jackson looks at me with raised eyebrows. "And this is a good holiday memory?"

I let out a laugh. "I know how it sounds, but that year, we

had the best apple pie of our lives, and we sat at the table at the Mitchells' that Thanksgiving telling this story about how miserable it was and how mom had forced us to go on this horrible road trip. We laughed our asses off the entire time, and we still can't tell that story without smiling." I shrug. "Sometimes, unexpected things can turn into the best memories, and to this day, Rusty has me make mom's apple pie every Thanksgiving."

He smiles at me, and there's something so sweet and genuine about it. "That's a really great story."

I nod. "It is."

We sit in silence together for a few minutes, each of us just watching the rotating pattern of tree lights—blue, green, white, red.

"What about you?" I end up asking a while later. "What's your favorite holiday memory? I know you said things are more nontraditional, but there has to be something you can look back on and say…that was the best Christmas or the best Easter or the best Arbor Day."

Jackson chuckles lightly but then goes quiet for a long time. So long, I wonder if maybe he's fallen asleep.

"Someday, when I look back on all the holidays of my life," he says, looking over at me, "I'll remember the one when I spent a few weeks in a tiny town in the mountains. I'll think to myself, the best holiday I've ever had was the night I sat under the tree lights drinking hot chocolate with Abby Fuller."

The small smile on my face falls away as surprise ripples through my body.

I assumed he'd tell me about traveling to a gorgeous hideaway in Aspen or spending his Christmas in the Caribbean. Something fantastic and fun and light.

I could never have guessed he'd share something as…unexpected as that. Something so honest. So vulnerable.

"I don't know. Maybe I shouldn't be saying something like that, especially when I promised your brother I'd be here for the business and only the business." He shakes his head. "But there is just something about you that feels different. Makes me want to reconsider…everything."

I swallow, tucking my leg against my body and wrapping my arms around my knee.

Jackson leans closer so our faces are just inches apart.

He stays there for what feels like forever, his eyes tracking between mine, then looking down at my lips. One hand comes up to the side of my face, and he leans in.

But instead of my mouth, I feel him press his lips against my forehead.

"Merry Christmas, Abby," he whispers.

Then he pulls back to look at me one more time before he gets up, puts his mug in the sink, and heads back upstairs.

chapter eight
Jackson

I stare out the window, drinking a warm cup of coffee mixed with just a bit of cream, as Abby and Rusty exchange gifts behind me. The two of them have been at it all morning, and it makes me smile.

Rusty explained to me yesterday that they give each other dozens of smaller gifts every year. The rule is that the gifts can't be more than ten dollars each, and they can only spend a total of two hundred dollars. Whatever else happens is up to them.

It's really a pretty cute system, and it's obvious they've been doing it for a while, considering the fact that each of them have been slowly buying gifts all year long. Just one of the many unique ways they've learned to be their own family.

"And this one is for Jackson."

I widen my eyes and turn around, surprised to hear that I've gotten a gift.

"What?"

Abby is looking up at me expectantly with her arm outstretched, a small box in her hand.

I glance at Rusty. "Did you have anything to do with this?"

He shakes his head. "Nope. Have no idea what's going on."

Setting my coffee down on the kitchen island, I accept the box from Abby and slowly begin to open the carefully wrapped present. It's solid white, barely larger than a phone, and when I slide the top off, I'm quite surprised at what I find inside.

Lifting the small rectangle out, I examine the words.

Cedar Cider Brewery and Pub, Jackson Page, Owner

It's a nametag made of wood, with the words burned in.

"I doubt you'll ever wear it," she says. "And maybe you already have a hundred things like that. But...I don't know. It seems like doing something like opening a brewery needs some sort of acknowledgment."

I look at Abby, feeling almost overwhelmed by her thoughtfulness.

It's been a long time since anyone bought me a Christmas present that wasn't liquor, gift cards, or something expensive that I didn't need or want.

This...

This is handcrafted. Thoughtful. Intentional.

It's beautiful.

"There's one for you too, Rusty," I hear Abby say, though her voice is kind of muffled as I continue to stare at her gift.

I just keep standing there, staring at it, feeling oddly choked up and emotional.

"Do you like it?"

I turn my eyes to where Abby is sitting on the edge of the couch, wearing those damn pink fuzzy socks and that same semi-see-through sleep shirt.

"I love it," I say, wanting to make sure she understands how much it means to me. "Thank you."

She bites her lower lip and gives me a soft smile before scooting back on the couch and snuggling up under a throw blanket.

"Now open this one," she says, pushing another box toward Rusty with her foot.

While her brother opens his next gift, I stare at Abby, feeling like I'm physically unable to look away.

Last night was more than a little surprising. I waffled for a good twenty minutes about whether or not I should come down when I heard her feet pad softly past my door, but I'm so glad I did. Talking with her last night, hearing her memories of her family…it made me seriously consider whether I'm missing something in my life.

I wasn't lying when I told Abby this Christmas has been my favorite holiday in memory, or when I said sitting with her in front of that tree last night will be the thing I look back on someday as my favorite holiday moment. The lights twinkling across her face, the way her eyes glowed as she talked about her parents…it was enough to make me realize that my feelings for Abby are growing a lot deeper and a lot more quickly than I ever could have expected.

And it's not only the physical, either. Abby isn't just someone I want to spread out naked and feast on every day. Well, actually, that's exactly what she is, but she's also a whole host of other things. She's kind and fun and outgoing and confident, not to mention beautiful as hell. Watching her play that card game last night, it was hard not to stare every time she laughed. That titter in her voice, the sparkle in her eye, the sheer joy on her face…I feel hooked.

With how I've felt about relationships in the past, these feelings bubbling up so soon and so intensely should make me want to get some distance, some perspective. Instead, all I can think about is drawing her closer, tucking her in under my arm and making her mine.

Which would make it difficult to keep my promise to Rusty.

"But your last gift is something we have to drive to go see."

I look back at where the two of them are seated on opposite ends of the couch, catching the quizzical look on Abby's face.

"What do you mean?"

"I mean exactly what I said. We have to get in the car and go somewhere for your final gift." Rusty smiles at her. "Let's go."

We move slowly as we try to get out the door—far too slowly for Rusty's liking if the way he's pushing us along is an indicator. Eventually, we're backing out of the driveway and heading off in what I think is the opposite direction of town.

"And you won't give me any hints?"

Rusty shakes his head. "Nope."

We drive for close to twenty minutes, looping most of the way around the lake until we pull into the driveway of a tiny bungalow.

Abby's eyes are narrowed as she stares at it. Then she turns to her brother. "What did you do?"

He shrugs and gives her a grin that's slightly goofy, then opens his door and gets out.

She glances back at me. "This is the place Briar and I are moving into on the first."

I nod, not having realized she was planning on moving out of the home she and Rusty currently share.

We get out of the car and take the path down from the driveway to the little house near the water. Then we follow Rusty as he leads us to the front door and opens it.

"How did you get a key?" Abby asks. "I don't even have a…"

But her voice trails off as she walks inside.

Following her in, I realize I have no idea what's going on, but clearly it's an emotional moment for her because Abby's on the verge of crying.

"You kept it?" she asks, her voice a whisper as a few tears streak down her cheeks. She bats them away as she looks around. "Seriously?"

"I was always the one who wanted to get rid of their stuff," Rusty tells his sister. "I knew you wanted to keep it, so…I put it in storage, figuring you could have it one day."

I stand off to the side, trying to stay out of the way as Abby wanders through the house, taking a look at all the furniture I'm guessing used to belong to their parents. A beautiful kitchen table and chairs. A wooden hutch. Bar stools.

When my curiosity gets the better of me, I peek down the hall and find Abby kneeling on the floor, her forehead resting against a wooden chest at the end of a queen-sized bed.

"This was my mom's," she tells me, stray tears sliding down her face. "She said it was a hope chest."

I don't know what that is, and seeing the confusion on my face, Abby explains.

"It's an old tradition. You get a hope chest when you're young, and you fill it with things for when you get married." Abby shakes her head and gives me a wobbly smile. "Mom never believed in that kind of thing, but she always said she liked the idea of a hope chest because it encouraged dreaming…planning for the future."

She looks at the top of the chest and rubs her hand along the grain of the wood.

"Now you can use it to plan for *yours*," I tell her, wishing there were some way I could alleviate her sadness but knowing there isn't.

She nods and gives me a sad smile. "Yeah. I can."

After another minute or so, I decide to step out of the house, feeling like I'm encroaching on something personal. Something precious. I take the short walk down to the dock that extends out into the water, my hands tucked into the pockets of my hoodie as I come to a stop at the end and stare out at the full expanse of Cedar Lake.

The evergreens stand tall and proud along the shore and rise up farther into the hills. It sure is a beautiful place to live, and I can't help but wonder what it looks like here when it snows.

When I hear the cadence of heavy footsteps behind me, I know it's Rusty coming up to stand with me on the dock.

"That's a pretty amazing gift," I tell him once he's at my side. "I almost cried myself."

I grin when I glance at him, trying to infuse a bit of levity into the moment, but it falls away when I see the way he's looking at me.

"I've been thinking about what I said the other night," he says, his jaw tight and his brow furrowed, his eyes lasering into mine. "About you only being here for the business and how we should pretend what happened between you and my sister didn't happen."

I swallow awkwardly, realizing if he's bringing it up, maybe this is a moment when I can talk to him about how I feel, tell him truthfully that…she's something pretty special.

Though I'm sure he's already more than aware.

"About that—"

"No, let me finish."

I twist my lips and nod, falling silent.

"I can't presume to know what's going on between the two

of you, and honestly, just thinking about my sister…" He pauses and shakes his head. "I just remember how we used to talk about the girls we'd hook up with in college, and the idea of her being one of those girls—"

"She's not, though," I say, interrupting him.

"I know." He sighs. "You didn't speak about her that way when you mentioned that you'd hooked up with someone at the resort." He takes a deep breath and lets it out. "I can't tell you how thankful I am that you didn't give me any details."

At that, I can't help but chuckle.

"I like her, Rusty," I tell him, shrugging a shoulder, knowing if I'm ever going to really say this right, it needs to be now. "I can't promise you I'm gonna marry her. I can't even promise that things will last longer than just the time I'm in town, but I *can* promise that the way I feel about her is…" I trail off, not even sure I know how I feel myself.

Rusty watches me for a second before his head bobs once. "Yeah, I figured."

He scratches at his beard and stares off into the distance for a minute before looking back at me.

"I guess all this is just me saying…you're adults. I don't get to have an opinion about who she wants to be with, and the same is true for you. So…" He turns to look me dead in the eye. "So I'd like to say this is my one warning, the whole 'hurt her and I'll fuck you up' thing big brothers do…but really, Abby can handle herself. I don't need to threaten you."

I grin at him. "Somehow, I don't doubt that she'll put me in my place if she needs to."

Rusty grins back at me. "Seems like you already know her a little better than I thought you did."

I snort and pin him with a look.

He closes his eyes and shakes his head. "That's not what I meant, Jackson."

"Yeah, I know. I'm just giving you a hard time."

We turn to walk back in from the dock, and Rusty pats me on the shoulder. It tells me we're going to be okay, him and me, our friendship. It says he trusts me. I like knowing I have his blessing, in a way. He's the family I've always wanted, and I couldn't imagine losing him.

Although, as we come up on the house and I see Abby stepping out on the deck, her eyes bright and a smile on her face, I know at some point I would have probably made a decision that jeopardized my friendship with Rusty. When I look at Abby, I feel like I finally understand what she was talking about earlier, about the hope chest.

But I don't need a physical box to place those dreams or hopes in. They can all wait inside my mind, nestled snuggly in the back, in a place I'm not yet ready to admit exists.

A place that, I think, belongs solely to her.

chapter nine
abby

The rest of Christmas Day goes by in a flash. After we leave the small house Briar and I are renting, we head home to take showers and get ready for the day. Then make our way down to the community center for Christmas dinner. It's one of the most beautiful things about living in Cedar Point and a tradition I haven't missed one single time, even during the years I was away for college.

It was started a long time ago, way before I was even alive, by the Mitchell family. Apparently, there was a Christmas back in the '50s when a lot of families in town were struggling to make ends meet. The Mitchells decided to do a big gathering for everyone in the town, not wanting to single out any of the families who wouldn't have been able to afford to put a meal on the table. Instead of doing it just the one time, it became a community tradition, and over the past few years, Patty has done a small speech reminding everyone of the importance of family and togetherness.

There are dozens of volunteers who help get everything ready to go the week before the event, and it is no easy task. Essentially, it's a buffet-style dinner served to anyone who is interested. Turkey. Stuffing. Mashed potatoes. Gravy. Mac and cheese. Green bean casserole. Bread. A few kinds of pie. Everyone brings their own plates and cutlery, as well as drinks and cups, and gets as many portions as they can handle.

Plates and cups in-hand and cutlery in our pockets, we walk the mile and a half from our house to Main Street, and I can't help but laugh at the confused expression on Jackson's face when we round the corner and come up on the hundreds of people spread all throughout downtown.

"Everyone's here for dinner?" he asks.

I nod, holding my plate against my chest as we get in line.

"We're all family," I tell him, smiling.

We spend a few hours downtown, eating, chatting, socializing with friends and neighbors. The tall space heaters spread along the walkway mixed with the body heat of so many people helps keep us warm until we decide to head home once the sun starts to set.

And then the three of us sit out on the couch and watch *It's a Wonderful Life* before going to bed.

I'm sure it seems like it's just a normal day, a normal Christmas, and by all accounts, it is. We exchange gifts. We go to dinner. We watch a holiday movie.

But through it all, my attention is hyper-focused on Jackson, on the smiles and winks he gives me and the easy way we seem to talk and flirt and laugh at every chance we get.

So, much later that night, after we've all been tucked away in our rooms for a while, I pad quietly down the hall and slip into Jackson's room. Closing the door behind me, I startle when

I find him sitting at the end of his bed.

"What are you doing?" I whisper.

"Trying to decide how long to wait for Rusty to fall asleep before walking to *your* room."

I smile at his response and cross to him, enjoying what it feels like when he pulls me against his chest and presses his lips against mine.

I planned on this being some tawdry rendezvous where I sneaked into his room and woke him up with my mouth between his legs, but this is so much better. These long, searching kisses and the way he has me wrapped in his arms make me feel like we're both lost in each other, like the only thing that exists is the way we're pressed together and held close.

It gives me a kick of hope that he's been feeling the same pull toward me all day as well.

Easing up after a few minutes, I rest my forehead against his, my breaths coming out in pants, my entire body ready to hop into bed and get the party started.

There's something I need to say first, but before I get the words out, Jackson speaks.

"Did you see outside?"

I pull my head back, my brow furrowed. "No."

He bites his lip and motions toward the window. Curious, I step out of his embrace and cross the room, a gasp falling from between my lips when I pull back the curtain and catch a glimpse of the white outside. A blanket of snow covers the ground in large patches and dusts the branches of the trees that stretch high into the darkened sky. But that beautiful, brilliant white catches the light of the moon and glows like something magical.

"I thought you said it normally doesn't snow here until January," he says, coming up behind me and wrapping his arms around my waist.

"That's because normally it doesn't." Pressing a hand against the window, I smile. "I can't even remember the last time it snowed on Christmas."

We stand there in silence for a long moment, each of us watching the flurries of white as they drift to the ground.

"I talked to my brother," I finally say, turning away from the window and looking up into Jackson's eyes. "I told him that who I want to sleep with…who I want to date or see or whatever…is up to me, and if that included you, it was my business."

He tugs me closer. "When was that?"

"Last night."

"What did he say?" he asks, grinning at me.

I shrug a shoulder. "Basically just that he's protective of me and remembers you being a playboy back in college."

That wipes Jackson's smile clean off his face. "I was, but I'm not anymore. It's been a long time since—"

I put a hand over his mouth and shake my head.

"You don't have to explain yourself. I'm just telling you what my brother said."

He shakes his head, dislodging my hand. "I talked to your brother too."

My eyes widen in surprise. "What? When?"

"This morning, on the dock. I told him…" He pauses. "I told him I like you and I would never hurt you, no matter what happens."

A small smile comes across my face. "And what did he say?"

"Basically, he said we're adults and could do what we want. Then he said he'd like to threaten me but that you could handle yourself."

I snort, loving how well my brother knows me.

"So what we're saying is basically that we each got my brother's permission to have sex."

Jackson's nose wrinkles and his lips scrunch up in displeasure. "Well that settles it—no sex tonight."

I burst into laughter, knowing it's probably loud enough to be heard through the door but choosing not to care.

"We can always have sex tomorrow instead," I tell him, slipping my hands underneath his sleep shirt and spreading my palms against his warm back. "I'm moving into my place with Briar a few days early."

"Oh yeah?"

I nod. "Rusty paid our landlord for an extra week so he could move the furniture in. That means I can start taking things over tomorrow morning."

"Won't you want to spend your first nights in your new place with your friend?" he asks, groaning slightly as I pop up to my toes and kiss his neck.

I shake my head. "Briar said she's still going to wait a few more days since she wants to spend time with her family." I shrug a shoulder. "She and I are both kind of late bloomers."

Jackson hums and bobs his head, considering. "Well, if you're inviting me over to have sex, I feel like the only polite thing to do is accept."

"But what if I don't want you to be polite?" I say, returning my mouth to his neck again.

He groans softly.

"What if I want you to be...unbelievably rude?"

"Fuck."

It's the only warning I get before Jackson is dragging me back to the bed and pressing his mouth against mine.

I want to moan and groan and sigh and whimper at the feel

of my body stretched out on the mattress next to his, but I know my brother is just across the hall. While we may have gotten his blessing in some weird capacity, I will happily draw a firm line in the sand at him overhearing me in bed.

We kiss for what feels like forever. In fact, it surprises me how long our mouths stay fused together, our tongues stroking against each other as we explore and tease and taste. It makes my mind cloudy, makes me feel like I could fall asleep right here next to him without anything else happening, and it would be enough.

"The way you kiss," he tells me—his hands coming up to hold the sides of my face—"it's fucking unreal."

I moan quietly in response, knowing anything I could say would be insufficient.

One more kiss on my lips before he's shifting us around so I'm lying on top of him with my face near his dick and my legs straddling his head.

"I've been wondering how you taste," he says, his words quiet.

And then, almost without warning, his thick tongue strokes into me, licks through the pool of wetness he helped create, from my clit to my core and then back. It's enough to have me shifting my hips, dropping my body slightly lower to give him better access so he can keep doing what he's doing.

"Clean and sweet," he mumbles.

He's sucking and licking and using his fingers to stroke and tug at the bundle of nerves that feels like it might burst at any moment. It feels so good, and I wriggle my hips, gyrating against him and enjoying the warm sucks and wet licks that are setting my body ablaze.

Dropping kisses along his pelvis, I take him in my hand

and stroke my tongue along the length of him. Then I bring the head of his dick into my mouth and suck, hard, before dropping down as far as I can go. He touches the back of my throat, and I swallow around him.

I can feel a change in him in that moment. The way he eats at me, the way his fingers slip into my core, the way his hips rotate and shift underneath me like he wishes he could hold me still and fuck into my mouth.

It makes me want to smile, knowing he's feeling that same clawing desperation I am. I can't smile, though, because I'm too busy sucking him in and shifting my own hips in quick circles as his mouth focuses almost entirely on my clit. All the while, one finger rubs and rubs and rubs on a spot deep inside me that has me digging my fingernails into his thighs with how impatient and on edge it makes me feel.

Before I tip over, he's shifting me off his body and climbing over me, reaching down to the ground to yank a condom out of his wallet. He gets it on in record time and then he's pushing inside me, so thick, so deep, so hard I can barely breathe.

It doesn't take long before my orgasm barrels through my body, and it's only seconds later that I hear him groan and feel him still on top of me.

We lie spent and panting until Jackson reaches down and tugs me up so I'm face to face with him, our naked bodies wrapped around each other in a way that feels intimate and warm.

"That was incredible," he tells me, dropping his mouth to kiss my neck. "You're incredible."

I stretch against him, enjoying the continued attention he wants to give me and dragging my short fingernails lightly up and down his back in a soothing caress. It isn't long before Jackson's movements start to slow, until I realize he's fallen asleep against me to the rhythm of my stroking along his back. I can't help the smile that takes over my face.

Who would have thought something as small as a quarter could have such a big part in bringing a man like him into my life? Jackson has been as much of a surprise this Christmas as that snow falling outside.

I don't know what's going to happen between us moving forward, whether or not this relationship is going to go anywhere, if it's going to fizzle out quickly.

Maybe we hook up a few more times but then realize we're not really compatible, or maybe we decide our playful nature together serves us better as friends than as lovers.

And then, of course, there's the chance that our meeting and instant attraction is just a taste of how good we can be together. That we're actually at the beginning of something special. The start of *someday*.

No matter what, I'm excited to explore. Excited to find out. Excited to have fun with the handsome man who's falling asleep in my arms.

And if it happens to become something more, I'll be excited for that too.

epilogue
jackson

"Happy New Year, Jackson."

I grin down at where Abby is tucked against me and drop a kiss to her lips.

"Happy New Year, Abby."

We both turn to look out over the lake, watching as the barge in the middle continues to shoot fireworks up into the air.

I've always loved fireworks. Ever since I was a kid, that whirring noise of anticipation then the explosion of light followed by the crackle as the flames in the sky fizzle into ash...it's always been the only thing I liked about the holiday season.

Year after year, I had subpar Thanksgiving and Christmas and New Year activities spent with people I knew but didn't feel particularly close with. Fireworks always felt like the payoff. If I could just get through the holidays, I'd get a light show at the end.

This year might be the first time I feel like the fireworks are just a distraction from the main event.

I wasn't expecting to find someone who makes me want more when I came on this short trip to Cedar Point, but Abby has done exactly that. Her positive energy, her loving spirit, her endless laughter… I can't get enough of it.

Over the past week, ever since our talk in my bed on the night after Christmas, we've pretty much been inseparable, apart from work. Though even then, we were still seeking each other out. I popped into the bakery to see her at least once a day, and she'd tag along with me and Rusty to wherever we needed to go to complete some of our business-related tasks.

At first, Rusty seemed somewhat wary of how quickly we'd clung to each other like magnets, but it only took a few days for him to realize how good we are together.

Because we are. Shockingly so.

And I couldn't be happier about it.

Which is why I've made a pretty big decision, though I haven't told Abby yet. I'm just hoping she's as happy about it as I am, because the wheels are already turning on this.

Once the fireworks are over, we head inside her new place, carrying in the two camping chairs we were using to sit in for a little while, as well as our beer bottles.

"Oh, hey, I just remembered," I say, holding up her set of keys. "Rusty told me I could give you your key back now that I've made my copy."

Abby glances back at me, a puzzled expression on her face. "Huh?"

"Now that I've used your key to make my copy," I repeat, waiting for her to understand what I'm saying.

"Why do you need a copy?"

"Wouldn't you want a key to your house?"

Her head tilts to the side. "But I *have* a key to my house. Do *you* need a key to my house?"

"It's my house too."

She stares at me for a moment longer, and then I see her face fall. For a split second, I worry I've made the wrong choice, worry I've misread her and she's wanting something more casual.

"Shut up."

I just watch her as she steps closer to me.

"I need you to explain yourself. Right now."

I nibble on my lip for a second before I just spit it out. "I'm moving into the guestroom at Rusty's," I tell her. "To be a full-time owner with him for the brewery."

"Are you serious?"

I nod.

"Seriously?"

Chuckling, I nod again.

Then, before I can say or do anything else, she hops up onto me, wrapping her arms around my neck and her legs around my waist.

"So you're happy?" I ask.

"Are you kidding me?" she shouts in my ear. She pulls back, and I finally see that brilliant smile I've been wanting. "Of course I'm happy."

I smile back at her, and then she's dropping her mouth to mine, giving me a kiss that tells me just how excited she is.

When I told Rusty I wasn't entirely sure where this was gonna go between Abby and me, I was serious. I didn't know—but I had an idea. Had an inkling. I could tell it was just…special. Different. Deeper, in a way neither of us was expecting.

So when it came time to decide whether I'd be buying a plane ticket to go home next week or sticking around Cedar Point to give this little town a shot at being my new home, there was no contest.

There's never been a contest, if I'm honest.

Abby and that damn quarter will win, every time.

And I wouldn't have it any other way.

For more stories from Cedar Point and the Mitchell family, visit my website:

www.jillianliota.com/cedar-point

jillian liota

acknowledgments
from the author

I've always wanted to write a holiday novella but for some reason, the right story has never felt within my grasp. Maybe it's because I'm a long-winded writer, but I've always found it challenging to convince a reader that love can happen in twenty thousand words.

Thankfully, when asked to join a holiday book box, I was in just the right place with my Cedar Point series to find the right words to tell the right love story.

First and foremost, thank you to my husband, **Danny**. We sat together to brainstorm and flesh this baby out when I was struggling with the concept that I just couldn't get right in my mind. Thank you for your beta reading, bike riding, book boyfriending perfection. None of my books would be complete without you.

Thank you to **Meredith Wild** for inviting me to be a part of the LuvBooks Holiday Box this year. You have been someone I've looked up to professionally for years, and it's been such a

jillian liota

pleasure to work with you. Thank you for the opportunity.

Mom, Dad, Caitlin, Kevin, Jordan, Cheyenne and **Mike,** I cherish each and every one of you. Thank you for your love and support.

Thank you to **C. Marie** for finding time in her super packed schedule to edit this story for me when the opportunity to write it came out of nowhere.

And to my **readers**: thank you for picking up the books I write, for being a part of my community, and for your constant, never-ending love affair with this series. Boyd and Ruby, Briar and Andy, and Jackson and Abby are just the first stories to come. There are so many more romances in Cedar Point that I can't wait to share with you.

Happy holidays and best wishes in the new year!

<3 always,
Jillian

Continue to the next page to read the first two chapters of

The Problem with Perfect

chapter one
bellamy

I stroll through the small group surrounding the fire, my hands tucked into the pockets of my jacket to ward off the light chill that clings to the air. It's the first bonfire night of the summer, the weather still a little crisp in the evenings and the crowd thin since not everyone has finished up the semester and traveled home from college yet. At the height of the summer season, there will be over a hundred people here, cars lined all down the dirt path leading into the closed-down campsite. But tonight, there are only about 20 or so folks scattered about, drinking and listening to music and reveling in the feeling of summer just on the horizon.

To be honest, I'm not really sure why I decided to come. I guess I feel bored…maybe a little impatient. It's this unfamiliar feeling that's been skittering beneath my skin recently, a sense of not knowing exactly what to do with myself. It's as if I'm just sitting around, waiting for life to happen.

Normally, I'm fairly relaxed, so this sensation is very unlike me. That's why I'm here, trying to find something to do, someone to talk to, something to take my mind off this feeling of stagnation.

My eyes scan the attendees littered around the gravel and dirt circle, taking stock of everyone and trying to decide who to approach. Unsurprisingly, most of the people here tonight are locals who graduated a few years before or after me. Familiar faces from around town, people I know of but don't really know.

Until my eyes halt on a familiar old Chevy Blazer in red with a white cover.

"What are *you* doing here?" I ask, my voice light and teasing as I approach the broad-shouldered back of a man I've known almost my entire life. "Aren't you too old to be at one of these things?"

Rusty pins me with an unimpressed look then returns to whatever he's doing at the tail end of his car. "I'm not here to party, Bellamy. Those days are in my past."

I snort and shake my head, watching as he tugs out a box of beer. "I didn't think you were here to party, Rusty. Besides, how long has it been since you graduated high school? Twenty years?"

He pauses and looks back at me over his shoulder with narrowed eyes. "Fourteen." Then he gives me his back again.

"Same thing." I lean against the Blazer and kick one foot over the other, tilting my head up to look at the sky, the stars slightly obscured by the smoke rising in the clearing between the trees.

I hear Rusty snort. "It is most certainly *not* the same thing." He passes by me and thunks a box onto the hood. "I thought you were supposed to be good at math."

I ignore his comment.

"So, what exactly *are* you doing here tonight?" I ask. "Because it looks like you're planning to dole out booze to Cedar Point's youth. Does Boyd know you're selling your product at the bonfire?"

He lets out an irritated sigh. "I'm not selling beer to Cedar Point's *youth*, Bellamy. Everyone is of legal age. A sale is a sale, and someday, when you've moved out of that plush house your parents own and you actually *need* the money you work for, you'll see what I mean."

I roll my eyes, not surprised by his bristly attitude. Rusty's always been that way—angry at the world. I don't make that statement with judgment; it makes sense considering the shitty hand life has dealt him. Still, it's rare for me to see him talk to anyone without a scowl on his face, besides his younger sister, Abby, and my brother, Boyd. The two of them have been friends since they were really young, which is why I'm not intimidated by his irritable bear act the way everyone else in town is.

That doesn't stop me from noticing what a dick he can be sometimes.

"You know, you have a way of being incredibly condescending."

Rusty heaves one of the boxes up on his shoulder then grabs the other and slides it forward until it's tucked against his hip.

"I *do* know. I figure it's the best way to keep you from annoying me with your jabs about how old I am." He starts walking away, heading over to where Corinne Paulson is standing with a group surrounding her dad's Saab.

I glare at his retreating form, cross my arms, and watch the slowly growing crowd. I've been here all of five minutes and it's easy to see that coming tonight was a mistake. Instead of chit-chatting and laughing with friends to distract myself, I'm stuck volleying insults with a guy who barely tolerates me.

Sighing, I push off of Rusty's car and round to the back, nosily eyeing the contents in the trunk: a few more beer boxes, what looks to be a box of tile samples, a flannel blanket, and—I huff a laugh.

A box of condoms. Classy.

I snag the box and glance inside, unsurprised when I see there's only one left. If I know anything about Rusty Fuller, it's that he is a man about town, and if I put stock in town gossip, it seems like he mostly gets his kicks with tourists passing through and looking for a good time with a guy who looks like a lumberjack.

Gross.

I could never sleep with someone like that—without emotion, without connection. Sex is special, something to be shared with people who mean something.

I glance back over to where Rusty is still talking with Corinne and roll my eyes at myself. Clearly it's time to leave. Standing around, snooping through the back of Rusty's Blazer is *not* what I had in mind for the evening. I should have just stayed home and done absolutely anything else until it was time to leave for my late shift at The Mitch.

Part of me thinks I should wait to say bye to Rusty, though I doubt he even cares. When I walk around to the front of the car, giving one final glance to the crowd before heading out, I hear my name in a familiar voice that has my heart swooping down into my stomach before launching itself into my throat.

Connor.

My eyes scan to the right until I spot him a few feet away, walking toward me, and I can't help the way a smile explodes on my face. God, I wish I could be more subtle, but that's just not how I was made.

"Hey, Connor!" I say, cringing only slightly at the overly enthusiastic way my voice has hit such a high note.

"Hey, Bells," he says, the sound of my nickname rolling off his tongue sending something warm through my chest. "You taking off?"

I shake my head, my plans changing on a dime now that Connor is here.

"No, I was just…"

But my voice trails off when I spot the body that emerges from behind him as he comes to a stop a few feet away.

As *they* come to a stop.

And I know instantly that they are a *they*.

She's beautiful. Short, thick, brunette hair that flips in a little bob around her jawline and wide beautiful eyes.

"Hey, Rusty," Connor says, and I glance briefly to the side, spotting Rusty's approaching form.

"Pruitt." Rusty's response is just as gruff as always.

I can't do anything except stare wide-eyed at Connor and the girl next to him…the one holding his hand.

"Hi, I'm Stace," she says, smiling at all of us. "Like Stacy, but without the *e* sound. Except my name ends with an *e* so…" She shrugs. "It can be *really* confusing."

I blink a few times then look at Connor.

"Stace, this is Rusty and Bellamy. Bellamy and I knew each other in high school."

Knew each other in high school. I almost want to laugh. That's how he wants to describe us? As people who knew each other in high school?

As if we don't know each other anymore?

As if we mean nothing to each other now?

"And Rusty owns Cedar Cider," he continues, "which is the best beer in town."

Rusty steps forward, and when I glance up at him, I see the tight smile on his face, his hands on his hips.

"Thanks for the compliment, Pruitt, and nice to meet you, Stace, but I need to take off."

"No worries, no worries," Connor says. "We can't stay long anyway. Just wanted to bring my fiancée by and introduce her to anyone who's back in town, though it looks like not too many people are out tonight."

I think that's what he says, but I can't be sure, because the ringing in my ears began when I heard him refer to Stace as his fiancée. I must stand there staring with my mouth agape for too long, because it isn't until I receive a physical nudge from behind me that I snap out of it.

"Huh?"

I glance at Rusty, who is looking at me with a quirked eyebrow.

"You alright?"

I look back at Connor, who is still watching me with an easy smile on his face like he hasn't just obliterated the very foundation of my heart.

"Yeah, sorry." I shake my head and try not to look like I'm dying inside. "What did you just say?"

"I said," Connor says slowly, "are you gonna be here a while? I was gonna walk Stace around…"

I clear my throat then shake my head. "I actually have to leave soon. I have… I'm closing at The Mitch tonight."

He bobs his head. "Yeah, okay. Well, we'll see you around. Maybe we can swing through later and grab a drink."

"Nice to meet you," Stace says, giving a friendly wave before she and Connor are turning and heading off toward a group of people a little ways away from us.

I watch them go, not even caring how awkward and weird I'm surely being by staring after them. Everything inside me feels dead. What the hell is happening? He's *engaged*? I didn't even know he was dating anyone.

My stomach rolls.

How long have they been together?

I spin around and put my back to the light of the fire, shielding my face from anyone who might be watching as a tear streaks down my cheek. I bat it away with the sleeve of my jacket, but just as quickly as the first popped up, another follows, and I know I need to get out of here immediately.

Without thinking, I walk to the passenger side of Rusty's car and tug the door open, climbing in next to him.

"What are you doing?" His question is tinged with that same irritation from earlier.

"I need a ride."

"Tough shit, Bellamy. I have somewhere to be."

I yank the seatbelt forward and click it into place.

"Please?" I ask, scrunching up my eyes trying to hold back the tears.

Rusty says something else—something equally as dismissive—and it's clear he doesn't want me here with him right now. But I don't hear him, because I bend forward and put my face in my hands as I burst into tears, my emotions slamming through me.

"I'm so sorry," I say, choking the words out between sobs.

I hear Rusty sigh and then feel the car begin to roll forward, hopefully carrying us far, far away from what is surely the worst moment of my life.

When I glance out the window 15 minutes later and see that he's pulled up outside The Mitch, my stomach turns over. I feel like I can barely breathe right now, let alone go in for a closing shift where I might have to face Connor and Stace later on top of dealing with every drunk in town.

Though downing a bottle of tequila sounds like it might be a good idea.

"Can you just take me home?" I ask, my voice small.

"I literally just drove you in the *opposite* direction of your house. You couldn't have said that earlier?"

"I'm sorry, I was..." But I don't get the sentence out before my eyes scrunch up and I break into tears again.

I hear him grumble something about my brother, then the car moves forward, through the gravel of the dirt lot and back out onto the main road. He doesn't turn in the direction of my house on the other side of the lake, though. Instead, he drives the few minutes back into town and then out onto the road that exits Cedar Point and leads down the mountain. It only briefly occurs to me to ask where he's going, but I resolve to just sit in silence and wait until he eventually takes me home.

I've never missed a shift before, so when I text my co-worker Emily to let her know I'm not feeling well and won't be able to head in, it only takes a split second before I get her reply saying she can cover for me, which I appreciate since I've covered for Emily on many, many occasions.

The tiny distraction her text provides is gone in a blink, leaving me with a stark reminder of what I learned tonight.

Connor has a fiancée.

Thinking about it again sends another wave of tears to my eyes, but this time I manage to sit and cry silently as Rusty drives us along the winding road out of town.

Connor was just here, in Cedar Point, not even three months ago for his mother's birthday. He came into The Mitch, sat at the bar, and talked with me all night like nothing had changed between us since last summer. He did that thing, the tucking my hair behind my ear thing that he's always done. Maybe I'm just incredibly naïve, but I feel like that's way too intimate of a thing to do to someone who is not your fiancée when you're engaged.

My train of thought is cut off as we come to a stop. I sit up straighter, wondering where we are. I've driven up and down this mountain for my entire life and have never stopped here before, at what looks to be a random turnout about ten minutes from town.

When I glance at Rusty, he's staring out the windshield, his jaw tight and his hands squeezing the wheel like he's hoping to rip it out.

A few minutes go by, and we just sit in silence.

Five minutes.

Six.

Seven.

Then, without a word, Rusty shifts the car out of park and turns us around to head back into town. I glance back, wondering what the hell that was abou…

And then it hits me.

I look at Rusty where he sits, taking in the emotion that's rolling off of him in waves. Today is the anniversary of when his parents died, when they were run off the road by a drunk driver just a few minutes outside of town.

It was the most horrible kind of tragedy. Cedar Point was devastated. Rusty and his sister Abby barely held it together. I was pretty young at the time—junior high, I think—but I remember the service like it was for someone in *my* family. It was the very first time I'd been to a funeral, and it left a mark I've never been able to wipe clean.

I want to say something to him.

Anything. Anything at all that might soothe him or ease some of the pain I'm sure he must be feeling, but I've never been good with words. I never know what to say or how to make anything better. Instead, somehow, I always seem to say something that makes it worse.

It's why I like numbers. There's no emotion in numbers, always a right answer.

With people, with situations like this, there's always the probability to get it wrong, and I hate to be wrong. I stay silent, eyeing him frequently as he drives us back into town and up the east side of the lake toward my parents' house.

"You gonna be okay?" he asks once he pulls into our driveway and comes to a stop.

I nod and try to give him some kind of smile. "Yeah. I'll be…" But a wave hits me, and I break into tears again. "I'm so sorry," I say, dropping my face into my hands again. "I feel so stupid crying about this when you're actually dealing with real pain, but I can't help it."

Rusty sighs, and then I'm startled by the feeling of a big, warm hand patting me roughly on the back. I glance up at him in surprise, catching the uncomfortable look on his face as he tries to console me, and my tears are brought to an abrupt halt as I burst into laughter.

He immediately withdraws his hand, but I keep laughing even as his eyes narrow at me.

"Why are you laughing?"

"Because…" My words come out in chunks as I continue shaking. "That was…the most awkward…consolation…back pat…to ever occur."

Rusty rolls his eyes and sits silently as I finish laughing, and when I finally trail off and wipe my eyes—this time from laughter and not from crying—I let out a long sigh and sag back into my seat.

"At minimum, thanks for the laugh. I needed it."

He makes some sort of sound that's reminiscent of a grunt of affirmation.

I grab my purse off the floor and push the door open but then turn to look at Rusty before I hop out. "I'm sorry if I ruined your evening, your plans to go…" I wave my hand, gesturing vaguely as if that can encompass *anything* about what his plans were tonight.

He shrugs a shoulder. "It's alright."

Nodding, I reach out and place my hand on his where it sits on the stick shift and give it a squeeze.

"See you around, Rusty."

The man bobs his head once and gives me a tight smile, and I take that as my cue to get the hell out of his car and out of his hair. I head into my dark house and up to my childhood bedroom, and I cry myself to sleep.

chapter two
rusty

"It looks great."

My eyes scan the structure, impressed by the work that has been accomplished in just the past six weeks. The rotting wood panels on the exterior have been treated and repaired in a way that preserves the look and feel of an old barn without the worries that come along with an antiquated building. The concrete flooring has been poured and finished, the interior re-insulated, and the windows and doors replaced. She looks brand-new but still beautiful and classic in a way that preserves the older vibe.

It's the one thing Jackson has nailed down that's of primary importance: we need to keep as much of the original structure as possible. Apparently old things are much more attractive than new things in the brewery space.

It speaks to the hipster soul.

My eyes nearly rolled right out of my head at that, but I just went with it because my business partner is nothing if not knowledgeable about this kind of shit. I, on the other hand, am

focused almost exclusively on the product, on the actual beer
we brew. It's been my baby for the past ten years and is where I
tend to focus the majority of my time and energy.

I don't care what Jackson says about the fact that people
will buy anything if you market it right. If I don't believe in
what I'm selling, I'm doing something wrong, and I know
without a shadow of a doubt that Cedar Cider is a top-notch,
quality craft beer.

"I'm glad to hear that," says our contractor Nick, a smile
on his face as he leads me around to the front again. "We've
been pushing to make up for the time we lost in March."

I nod. We had an unexpected dumping of snow in early
March that took a few weeks to melt off, and that delayed the
project start date. I know construction jobs always come up
against hiccups and delays, but I wasn't expecting to face such a
big one right from the jump.

Thankfully, Nick is the kind of guy who *also* isn't a fan of
delays, and I've been pleased to see just how aggressively he's
tried to recoup the lost time.

"What's the timeline for installing the brewing equipment?" I step through the open doorway to the main space,
looking at the long wall where the majority of the distillers will
be lined up as a backdrop for the bar.

"By July at the latest. We're going to stick with setting up
the interior in phases, like we discussed, and we need to get the
kitchen elements in first before we bring in such large equipment. Otherwise it'll be a game of 'will it all fit', which is just a
waste of time for everyone."

I cross my arms, mulling it over. I communicated that the
brewing equipment needed to be in as early as possible so we
could begin using it. Ideally, I'd have liked three months with it

before we open in September, but I guess two will have to do.

"Alright, well, keep me posted about how things progress."

We shake hands. "Always."

I head back to my Chevy, leaving Nick and his crew behind to continue the final window installation that's happening today. I hop into the driver's seat and pull out my phone.

Me: Things are going good. We'll be able to finalize the equipment order in the next few weeks.

Almost instantly, I see the bubbles that mean Jackson is responding.

Jackson: Awesome. I'll set up the meeting with Harold.
Boyd: Harold's the guy from BruWorks?
Jackson: Yeah.
Me: And you're still sure BruWorks is who we should work with? Because I've been using Master Brewer for ten years.

We've had this discussion a few times, and I've asked for him to confirm and reconfirm the reasons behind why he thinks BruWorks is the better company to purchase our new, much larger brewing equipment from.

Jackson: Yes. I am.

I can almost hear his irritation through the text, but I can't help it. I'm not great with change. I'm not the kind of guy who jumps on the new hot thing that's changing the game. I'm the guy who sticks with one thing for decades.

Deodorant.

Cereal.

Windshield wiper fluid.

Brewing equipment is no different, and I've been using Master Brewer since I first started brewing in my garage, though with a much smaller setup. I did it as a way to distract myself after I moved back to Cedar Point, and now their machinery is so intrinsic to me that switching manufacturers feels like a punch to the gut.

But Jackson is more than just my roommate and college buddy. He's one of my business partners for a reason, and I trust him. I trust not only his knowledge and experience but his intuition as well. So if he says it's the right move, I need to trust that, too.

Me: Sounds good. Just let me know when.
Jackson: Will do

I drop my phone into the cup holder, pulling out of the gravel lot and down the dirt road that's just off the end of Main Street and heading back into town. Today is a lot busier than I thought it was going to be, and I still have quite a few deliveries to make, both here in Cedar Point and throughout several of the small mountain communities nearby that keep Cedar Cider stocked in their convenience stores and restaurants. Nobody told me how much driving would be involved in keeping a small brewing business afloat. Most days I feel more like I'm delivering pizza than crafting beer.

I back my car into a spot behind One Stop Shop and pop the trunk, where I have ten cases of beer waiting to be unloaded. Thankfully, I was able to partner with a distributor who manages all the restocking down the mountain at the locations

that keep our beer on the shelves, but for all the little businesses up here in the mountains, the cost of hiring someone else is
just too great, so I handle those deliveries myself, including our
local grocery, One Stop.

I push through the back door and prop it open then grab a
dolly and begin unloading the first five boxes.

"Hey man."

I look over my shoulder and grin when I spot Andy Marshall, clipboard in hand, standing in the doorway.

"Happy Monday."

I snort. "Mondays are never happy."

He flashes me a smile and moves out of the way as I wheel
the dolly into the stock room in the back of the store.

"I love Mondays."

"That's because you take off Tuesday and Wednesday," I
reply. "I'd love Monday too if it was the start of my weekend."

He laughs and follows behind me as I head into the main
store and over to the beer fridge. "Yeah, okay. I guess that
makes sense." He pauses. "I was thinking about you yesterday."

I glance back at him just as I yank the fridge door open,
unsurprised when I see the sympathetic look on his face. Andy's
always been a softy at heart, and he tells me some version of the
same thing every year at this time. He knows I don't want to
talk about it.

Nodding, I don't address what he said, making quick work
of hoisting the cases onto the appropriate shelves.

"What did you get up to this weekend?" I ask once I
emerge and see that he's waiting for me. "Did Briar have that
thing?"

He shakes his head and follows me as I head back to my
car for the second load. "It's this coming weekend. We're head-

ing down to Sacramento tomorrow for a few days, gonna make a little trip out of it."

"Sounds fun."

"I hope so."

Andy's girlfriend Briar is an exceptional florist, and she's competing in some kind of regional bouquet contest. She's been talking about it for months, sharing all the things she's been doing to prepare.

It's wild to me the things people find interesting. The idea that there are enough people into putting together vases of fancy flowers to the point that there are regional competitions... ones that lead to state and national competitions...it's just mind-blowing.

That said, I'm sure there are things I do that other people are shocked by. Well, things I *would* do if I had time to have any hobbies. Right now, nearly every minute goes into my business, whether it's day-to-day ops or working on something for the opening. Besides one or two other responsibilities, I just don't have time for anything else.

Besides, I'm not really a joiner, not a hobby kind of guy. I mean, I can't even imagine what I'd look like doing...something else, like playing tennis or collecting coins.

A huff of laughter falls from me as I finish up with the delivery and sign the paperwork with Andy that reflects the quantity of items I stocked up.

"I was thinking about heading into The Mitch tonight, grabbing a beer. You interested?"

I close the trunk of my car, considering. I'm a regular there, but I'm not really in the mood for being friendly.

It's almost like Andy can read my mind.

"We do this song and dance every year, Rus. You don't have

to talk to me. You can just be a grump, but you shouldn't be alone right now."

I grind my teeth together a little bit, considering. He's right. I know he is.

So I nod. "Yeah, just text me what time."

Andy slaps my back and gives me that stupid smile again. Sometimes I wish I could be a happy man like Andy is, someone who sees the positives in things and stays optimistic, but I just don't have it in me.

I'm not sure I ever have.

When I walk into The Mitch later that evening, I pause in the entry like I do nearly every time, allowing my eyes to adjust to the dim lighting. This place is the quintessential dive bar, complete with a dart board, a pool table, a juke box, and a hazy quality that makes it seem like people still smoke inside even though that's been banned since before I was legal to drink.

Once I can see, it only takes a second to scan the room and realize Andy hasn't arrived yet. I cross to the bar and slip onto a stool, ordering a whiskey neat from the bartender—Emily, I think?—a cute blonde who's wearing the employee shirt that says *Mitch Bitch*.

She gives me a look I know well—one that tells me I can have more than just the drink if I ask—before striding down to the other end of the bar to attend to other patrons. If Emily were on *this* side of the counter, I'd be taking her up on whatever that look might promise, but I've learned well enough not to mess around with locals.

What's that old saying? Don't dip your pen in company ink? It's like that, but with the town, which is why I don't flirt or fuck with people who live here. Not anymore. The last thing I need is some sort of drama when I ultimately don't want anything more than a good time.

I *used* to hook up with fellow townies, but my sister begged me for years to stop sleeping with people we know, and after one particularly bad experience involving a woman who wasn't as single as I assumed, I decided she was right. Who needs a black eye anyway? Besides, it's much cleaner to sleep with people who aren't planning on sticking around.

My phone vibrates on the bar, and when I glance down, I see Andy's text on the screen.

Andy: Sorry, man. Got tied up. Be there in 20.

Twenty minutes isn't that long, but it's just another chunk of time for me to wish I were back at my own house, where the whiskey is significantly cheaper. I pick up my Woodford and take a sip, enjoying the burn as it coats my mouth and runs down my throat, before staring blankly into the glass.

Has it really been ten years?

I seem to ask myself that question every year on the anniversary of their death. Each one seems almost unbelievable, but ten is a milestone. A decade. The idea that it's been *a decade* since I've talked to them is just…

A laugh catches my attention, pulling me from my memories and the emotional place I almost slipped into. I glance over to where Emily is talking with Bellamy Mitchell, the latter tying an apron around her hips, a wild smile on her face. When Bellamy's eyes catch mine, her laugh fades, replaced almost immediately by a look of embarrassment. She says something else to the blonde and then heads my way.

Another perk of drinking at home alone—I don't have to worry about bumping into people I don't feel like talking to in the exact moment I don't want to talk to them. It's not that I have anything against Bellamy, exactly, but the last thing I want is for her to rehash whatever that was last night, aka the weirdest hour I've ever experienced.

"Hey, Rusty," she says, planting her hands wide on the bar top and leaning forward. "About last night…"

"Don't worry about it," I tell her, because I don't want to talk about it.

"But I've been feeling awkward about it, and I just wanted to say I'm sorry."

"You already apologized. No need to do it again."

Her nose scrunches up. "I get that, but I still feel like an absolute ass. I mean…" She sighs. "You were going through something, and I was—"

"Bellamy."

Her warm chestnut eyes, which always seem far too trusting for her own good, blink a few times at my interruption.

"It's fine."

She nibbles on her lip and, begrudgingly, bobs her head a few times.

"Alright. If you're sure."

"I'm sure."

"Well…thank you again. For the ride home and the…consolation."

At that, she gives me a real smile, and I fight the urge to do the same as she begins to giggle. Her mouth opens slightly, like she's about to say something else, but a look of…I don't know, something uncomfortable overtakes her for just a moment. Then a big fake smile stretches wide on her face.

"Hey there, Bells."

Connor Pruitt walks up to the bar and hops onto the stool next to mine.

"Hi Connor. What can I get you?"

My eyes scan over Bellamy, taking in the stiff way she's standing, her hands twisting together in front of her even as she pretends she's happy to see him.

"Just a Coors would be good."

Lifting my glass to my mouth, I fight the urge to sneer at him. Two dozen beers on tap, and he goes with Coors?

Bellamy makes quick work of snagging a glass and tilting it under the tap, her eyes zeroed in on where it slowly fills the pint.

"Hey, listen," Connor starts, and I already have a bad feeling about whatever is going to come out of his mouth just based on his tone. "I hope I didn't upset you the other night. With Stace."

Bellamy blinks a few times but keeps her gaze on the beer as she finishes pouring, sets a coaster on the bar, and thunks the glass down on top of it.

"What do you mean?" she asks, that same saccharine look on her face.

"Oh, you know, just…" He pauses and glances at me for a second but still continues. "…I know you've had, you know, a crush on me for a while…"

My eyebrows rise, and I watch as Bellamy's jaw drops just slightly.

"…and last summer was a bit of fun, for sure. But I just wanted to make sure you didn't take the news too hard. About the engagement."

A beat goes by. And then another one.

Suddenly, Bellamy breaks into laughter, but it's not her real laugh. No—her *real* laughter is that barely-breathing, gasping-for-air thing she did in my car last night, or the little giggle she just gave me a second ago.

This laugh is high-pitched and uncomfortable and draws the attention of just about everyone around us.

"Connor, you are so funny," she says, planting her hands on her hips. "I am not at *all* upset about you and Stace. I'm very happy for you."

I glance at the man next to me, and I can tell he's anything but convinced.

"Besides, I'm not sure my boyfriend would be happy to hear about this supposed crush," she continues, laughing dramatically again. "He'll get a hoot out of this story when I tell him."

Connor watches Bellamy with amusement, and it really pisses me off. Clearly, she's had feelings for this guy, and he's sitting here *enjoying* how uncomfortable she is about the whole thing, his engagement and whatever.

What a prick.

"I didn't realize you were dating someone," he replies, tilting his head and examining her. "Is it serious?"

She nods. "Very."

"Funny…I feel like someone would have mentioned if another one of the Mitchell girls got into a serious relationship. You should have heard my mom going on and on about Briar and Andy last year." He chuckles. "Drove Keegan nuts."

That's because your sister was trying to make a play for Andy, you dumb shit. That's what I want to say, but I keep my mouth firmly closed.

"Yeah, well…we've been keeping it under wraps, wanting to make sure it's real before we talk to anyone about it."

Connor nods, but it's clear he doesn't believe her. I don't envy her with this hole she's digging, and I can't imagine how she's going to climb her way out of it without making herself look…

"But I guess it's finally time to tell everyone, Rusty."

Her words cut my thought off in the middle, and I blink a few times, trying to understand what she just said.

"He's been so cautious," she continues. "Not wanting to upset anyone because of, you know, the fact that he's friends with my brother and everything. But, yeah…"

There's a beat of silence from Connor, and I just keep staring at Bellamy, who is looking at me with a hint of desperation clouding her eyes.

"*You're…dating…Rusty.*"

There's a thick layer of disbelief in Connor's voice, and when I finally turn to look at him, I see a completely different expression on his face than was just there a moment ago. Gone is the cocky, incredibly arrogant prick who was sitting next to me, and in his place is, well…still a prick, but one who looks a lot more uncertain. Almost like he doesn't like the idea of me dating Bellamy.

Well, I don't like the idea either, but I *do* like the idea of putting this little shit in his place. Before I can think better of it, I'm muttering two words I'm almost certain I'll regret.

"She is."

BELLAMY AND RUSTY'S LOVE STORY CONTINUES IN

the problem with perfect

AVAILABLE ON AMAZON AND KINDLE UNLIMITED

jillian liota

about the author
jillian liota

Jillian Liota is a Southern California native currently living in Suwanee, Georgia. She is married to her best friend, has a three-legged pup with endless energy, and acts as a servant to a very temperamental cat.

Jillian writes contemporary and new adult romance, and has had her writing praised for depth of character, strong female friendships, deliciously steamy scenes, and positive portrayal of mental health.

To connect with Jillian:

Join her **Reader Group**
Sign up for her **Newsletter**
Rate her on **Goodreads**
Visit her on **Facebook**

Check out her **Website**
Send her an **Email**
Stalk her on **Instagram**
Add her on **Amazon**

jillian liota

additional titles
from jillian

For an up-to-date list of titles, visit:
www.jillianliota.com/books

For bonus content, visit:
www.jillianliota.com/bonus